ON THE FLY

Visit us at www.boldstrokesbooks.com

Praise for PJ Trebelhorn

The Right Kind of Wrong

"[A] nice, gentle read with some great secondary characters, easy pacing, and a pleasant writing style. Something you could happily read on a lazy Sunday afternoon."—*Rainbow Book Reviews*

"PJ Trebelhorn has written a romantic, sexy story with just the right amount of angst."—*Kitty Kat's Book Review Blog*

"The love story between these two characters is well formed and you can understand their feelings for one another as well as knowing the inner turmoil of potentially losing your best friend."—*Les Rêveur*

From This Moment On

"*From This Moment On* is a fine read for coping with loss as well as being a touching lesbian romance tale."—*Midwest Book Review*

"Trebelhorn created characters…that are flawed, faulted, and wholly realistic: While many of the characters are struggling with loss, their unique approaches to dealing with it reveal their weaknesses and give the reader a deeper appreciation of the characters…*From This Moment On*…tells a gripping, emotional story about love, loss, and the fusion of the two."—*Philadelphia Gay News*

Desperate Measures

"I love kick-ass police detectives, especially when they're women. This book contains a superior specimen of the breed."
—*Rainbow Book Reviews*

Taking a Gamble

"This is a truly superb feel-good novel. Ms Trebelhorn is obviously an accomplished writer of engaging and riveting tales. Not only is this a very readable novel but it is full of humour and convincing, beautifully written and conceived realities about falling in love for the first time."—*Inked Rainbow Reads*

By the Author

ON THE FLY

by

PJ Trebelhorn

2018

ON THE FLY

ISBN 13: 978-1-63555-255-3

THIS TRADE PAPERBACK ORIGINAL IS PUBLISHED BY
BOLD STROKES BOOKS, INC.
P.O. BOX 249
VALLEY FALLS, NY 12185

FIRST EDITION:SEPTEMBER 2018

CREDITS
EDITOR: CINDY CRESAP
PRODUCTION DESIGN: STACIA SEAMAN
COVER DESIGN BY SHERI (HINDSIGHTGRAPHICS@GMAIL.COM)

Acknowledgments

I've loved the game of ice hockey for as long as I can remember. My uncle Tom took me to my first Portland Buckaroos game when I was about seven, and I was hooked for life. When they left Portland, we were without a team for about three years until junior hockey finally came to town. Even though I live in New York now, I still follow the Portland Winterhawks, a junior team in the Western Hockey League (WHL), one of three leagues under the umbrella of the Canadian Hockey League (CHL) mentioned in this book. Unfortunately, I never learned to ice skate, so I never played the game, but I always dreamed of what it would have been like to play.

I want to thank everyone at Bold Strokes Books for being so wonderful to work with, especially Sandy Lowe and Radclyffe. I'm proud to be a part of the BSB family.

Thanks also to my editor, Cindy Cresap, for making it look like I know what I'm doing. Your humor and insight are amazing.

Thanks to my sister, Carol, for continuing to be my biggest cheerleader. Also to Susan and Harvey Campbell for being two of the best people I know.

A big thank you to my wife, Cheryl, for always supporting me and understanding my need to write. You truly are the best thing that's ever happened to me.

But the most important thank you goes out to you, the reader. I love hearing from you, whether it be through email or messages and posts on Facebook. As long as you keep reading, I'll keep writing.

For Cheryl, always

CHAPTER ONE

S hit," Courtney Abbott muttered under her breath as she picked herself up off the ice again. She glared at the woman who'd driven her hard into the boards and took a couple of strides toward her.

"What's the matter, Abbott?" Jen Hilton asked, a wicked grin showing through the cage covering her face. "Are you finally realizing you're getting too old for this?"

Court dropped her stick and moved toward her again, taking satisfaction in watching as Hilton's grin slowly disappeared. She was getting tired of this rookie pushing her buttons. Maybe it was time to teach her a lesson.

Their coach, Gail Crawford, blew her whistle and quickly skated over to stand her ground between them. "Are you ladies finished? You know this is supposed to be a practice, right? Court, I need you in the lineup tomorrow night—not sitting in the stands with an injury that could have easily been avoided."

"It's all good," Jen said as she skated backward and tapped her stick on the ice a couple of times. Court stayed in place and watched her, hoping like hell she'd fall on her ass. "Come on, Abbott, let's show them how it's done."

This was a taunt, something Court was used to from the younger players who thought their shit didn't stink. She looked around at her teammates, who were all watching the exchange with a little too much interest as far as Court was concerned.

"We're done for today," Gail said after a moment. When no one moved to leave the ice, she turned and looked at all of them. "What the hell are you waiting for?"

They all skated away, and when Court started to follow them, Gail grabbed the sleeve of her jersey, effectively stopping her.

"Hold up a second, Court," she said.

Court turned and met her eyes. They'd known each other for years, since before Court even started playing hockey. Gail had been the older sister of one of Court's best friends when Court was eight years old and Gail was fifteen. The best friend of her youth, Gail's little sister Jeanine, dropped out of Court's life when she came out to her at sixteen. Gail had always been there for her, though, and Court was forever grateful for her support.

"What?" Court asked, feeling a bit snippy. She shoved her right glove under her arm and pulled her hand out of it.

"What the hell's going on between you and Hilton?"

"You should ask her, because I seriously have no clue."

"Look, I know she has a chip on her shoulder, but she could be the future of this team," Gail said. Court shook her head and looked down the ice toward the empty net.

"I know, but Jesus, Gail, she's an ass." Court knew Jen Hilton could be the future, but knowing it was true didn't make it any easier to swallow. "But right now, I'm still here, and I have two years left on my contract. I'm thirty-four years old. I know I'm not going to be playing this game forever, but I'd like to enjoy the time I have left."

"Christ, you make it sound like you're in the death throes."

Gail laughed as she started to skate slowly toward the bench. Court matched her stride for stride.

"It kind of feels like it sometimes." Court playfully nudged her with an elbow before unsnapping her chinstrap and removing her helmet. She handed it to Gail and ran a hand through her sweat-soaked hair. "If I was, it would certainly make Hilton happy."

"No doubt, but you need to find a way to work with her, Court." Gail stopped before stepping off the ice. "You need to teach her the ropes."

"Like hell, Gail," Court said, sounding as whiny as she had when she was ten. "She thinks she knows everything there is to know about everything already. I can't teach her anything."

"You need to try," Gail said softly. "It isn't me. This is coming from the front office."

"Fuck." Court took her helmet back with a little too much force.

"Hurry up and get showered," Gail said. "You and I are going for pizza. My treat."

Court nodded and headed for the locker room. She breathed a sigh of relief as she sat on the bench in front of her locker and leaned down to unlace her skates. She hoped Jen was gone and not simply in the shower, because the woman seriously rubbed her the wrong way. Sure, Court had been young once too, but she didn't think she was ever as brash as Jen Hilton.

Playing professional ice hockey had been Court's dream for as long as she could remember. Of course, she'd always thought she might be able to break into the men's game, but she was convinced now it would probably never happen for a woman. So she was grateful there were small women's leagues popping up over the years to give young women the opportunity to play other than just for a national and an Olympic team.

The league she played in consisted of eight teams, and she'd played her entire career with the Kingsville Warriors. She'd also been in two Olympics and had two medals to show for it, one of them gold and the other a bronze. Playing professional women's hockey was never going to make her rich, though. Her day job was being a Realtor, which was okay and more than paid the bills, plus it was flexible enough to allow her to play hockey. If she had a game, or a practice, she just didn't schedule any appointments during a time that might interfere. But she so wanted hockey to be her career in some way, shape, or form.

"Wake up, Abbott," Jen said with a slight shove to her shoulder, her hair still wet from the shower. "Is it past your bedtime?"

Court said nothing in response, but simply went about removing her jersey and pads. She knew Jen saw her silence as a sign of weakness, but she didn't really care. Jen could think whatever she wanted.

"Hilton, back off," said Charlotte Lincoln, their starting goaltender. She was young too, but she wasn't full of herself like Jen. Court liked her.

"This is none of your business," Jen told Charlotte without looking away from Court.

Court stood, and she felt a small amount of satisfaction when Jen took a step back from her. Being almost six feet tall was an advantage at times like these.

"You have a problem with me, Abbott?" Hilton asked.

"Nope," Court replied with a shake of her head and a slight curve of her lips. "I don't have a problem with anybody. I'm the most laid-back person you'll ever meet."

"Truth!" a couple of women a few feet away from them

called out. Court smiled to herself and grabbed the shampoo from her locker. The Warriors were a family, and Court loved how they stuck up for each other, on or off the ice.

Court was a bit surprised when Jen turned her back and started getting things from her locker so she could leave. Why was she backing off so easily? *I don't trust her.* Court slammed her locker shut and headed for the shower.

"Maybe your teammates would be interested in knowing they're sharing a shower with a lesbian."

There it was. The idiot kid who thought she could get under Court's skin. Better people had tried and failed over the years. She turned back and faced her, but her line mate, right winger Savannah Wells, shoved Hilton hard against the locker. Court stayed where she was. Court was the captain of the team, but there were some things she'd rarely get involved in. Especially when there was someone who needed to be put in their place.

"Listen, you little bitch," Savannah said, getting right into her face. "Most of us have been playing together for longer than you know. If you think any of us didn't already know that about our captain, then you're more stupid than I thought."

"And she's not the only one, Hilton," a voice said from the other side of the room. Court looked at her left wing Kelly Rawlins, and they smiled at each other. "So you might want to watch what you say, and who you say it to."

Court went to the showers. Her family had her back.

By the time she emerged from the shower, a towel covering her body, Jen Hilton was long gone. Savannah and Kelly were waiting for her at her locker, though.

"Please tell us the Warriors are going to use her as trade bait," Savannah said.

"I wish I could," Court answered as she pulled on her underwear and a pair of jeans. She rubbed her hair with a towel she then tossed into the dirty laundry bin before quickly putting on her bra and pulling a T-shirt over her head. She finger combed her hair and took a seat to put her shoes and socks on. "You know as well as I do they think she's the future of this team."

"Fuck," Kelly said. "We have good chemistry on this team. Why do they want to mess with a championship roster?"

"None of us are getting any younger," Court said, pointing out the obvious. "You have to make changes so the team doesn't suffer."

"What if the team suffers *because* of the changes?" Savannah asked, looking pissed off.

"We've all dealt with women like her in our careers," Court told them. "And they generally settle down and become productive and valuable parts of the team."

"Why are you defending her?" Savannah asked, looking as though her head might explode. "She ran you hard into the boards in a *practice*, Court, and then continued to ride you here in the locker room. That is not acceptable."

Court shoved her equipment into her athletic bag and shut her locker. They played their games in this arena but didn't have a dedicated locker room. Other teams and even the public used them during the times they weren't scheduled to either play or practice, so they couldn't leave anything behind. She hefted the huge bag and slung it over her shoulder before turning to face them.

"She'll either mature, or she'll get what's coming to her from someone on another team," she said quietly. She shook her head because she so wanted to be the one to put her in her place, but knew that line of thinking would get her nowhere. "Just let it go, okay, guys? As far as I'm concerned, at this point in her career, she isn't worth a suspension or having one of our contracts bought out. We need to show her through our actions how she should carry herself."

Her teammates stood in defiance for a moment, but they finally nodded their agreement. Court breathed a sigh of relief.

"You want to go out with us tonight?" Kelly asked. "There's going to be a lot of women at the bar."

"No, not tonight," she answered as she headed toward the door. "I'm going for pizza with Gail, and probably her family too. I'll see you guys tomorrow."

CHAPTER TWO

L ana!" Joey yelled from the kitchen. She stopped what she was doing—getting a customer a pitcher of beer—and looked back at him. "Order up!"

Lana Caruso sighed in frustration. He couldn't have waited for her to finish with the beer? Working in her family's pizzeria at the age of thirty-six wasn't what she'd ever thought she'd be doing, but her father had suffered a pretty major heart attack and Joey had asked her to come back home to help with things at the pizzeria. She'd never been able to say no to Joey. Unfortunately, that meant taking a leave of absence from her position as second violin in the Chicago Orchestra. And now, here she was, more than seventy miles from the nearest metropolis, and stuck in Kingsville, Pennsylvania, once again.

"I was helping someone, Joey," she said as she grabbed the pizza and walked away to deliver it to the table of hungry customers without waiting for a response from him. No doubt it would just be something likely to piss her off anyway. He should be grateful she was helping him out at all. Thankfully, the orchestra gig paid her well, and she had plenty of money saved. She just wasn't happy about making Eric change schools for the rest of the year. Also, living in the room she'd grown up in wasn't helping matters. At least she had an appointment in the morning with a Realtor to see about leasing a house.

Where the hell were all these people coming from anyway? It was a freaking Tuesday night, and she hadn't had an opportunity to even sit down for more than thirty seconds. She pointed at an empty table, a hot commodity apparently, for the two women who'd just walked in. They'd just have to wait for her to catch a minute to be able to take their order.

She finally made it to their table a few minutes later and held her order pad in front of her. She spoke without bothering to look at either one of them.

"What can I get you?" she asked, pen ready to start scribbling.

"Large pepperoni, please," one of the women said.

"Drinks?" Lana asked.

"A pitcher of whatever's on tap will be fine."

She put her pad in her front pocket and picked up their menus just as she looked at them and smiled. She faltered for a moment, hoping the two women didn't notice. She was looking into the bluest eyes she'd ever seen in her life. The woman smiled back at her, and Lana nodded once before walking away to put in their order.

The pizza gods seemed to be looking out for her, because the steady stream of customers they'd seen for the past couple of hours was finally slowing down. More people were leaving than coming in. Lana escaped to the kitchen and let out a deep breath.

"How you holding up?" Joey asked, wiping his hands on the towel he had hanging out of the front pocket of his jeans.

"How do you do this every night? And since when did this place turn into such a hotbed of activity?" Lana asked.

"You've seen the menu," he answered with a shrug. "Best pizza outside of New York City."

"Whatever." Lana rolled her eyes. Obviously, her brother knew nothing about Chicago deep dish. Now *that* was pizza. She stood and went to look through the pass to the two women waiting for their pizza. "Who are they?"

"Who?" Joey stood next to her, looking out at the dining room.

"Those two women over there." She pointed, and Joey followed her line of sight.

"Customers?" he asked with a grin.

"You're an ass." She threw an elbow to his side, making him wince.

"Sorry, sis, but I don't know them," he said as he went to check on what Lana assumed was their pizza. "They come in a lot, though, if that helps."

She watched the women while Joey sliced their pizza. They didn't look like they were together, and one of them appeared to be older than the other. The younger one might very well be the most attractive woman Lana had ever laid eyes on. Her light brown hair was cut short, above the neckline of the T-shirt she was wearing, but it was the gorgeous eyes holding her attention. They were so blue, Lana thought she could actually fall into them. She shook her head to dispel the thought as Joey shoved their pizza onto the counter in front of her.

She concentrated on making it to their table without dropping their pizza, because her knees were shaking, and she didn't know why. Well, she did, but she certainly didn't want this beautiful woman to know why.

"Here you go, ladies," she said as she set it on the table between them. She deposited some extra napkins as well before the older woman looked up at her.

"You must be Lana," she said, and then she laughed when

Lana was sure she had a look of confusion on her face. "Your brother said you were going to help him out here for a bit."

"Funny, but he told me he didn't know you," Lana said, risking a look over her shoulder. She saw Joey in the kitchen laughing. She was definitely going to kill him. She plastered a smile on her face and focused on her table again. "Yes, I'm Lana."

"I'm Gail," she said and held out her hand. Lana took it briefly before turning toward Gail's friend.

"Courtney," the other woman said, but then she smiled and shook her head. "Court."

Lana tilted her head to the side. "Really? Your parents named you Courtney Court? That just seems cruel." She winked at her, which caused Court to laugh, and Lana felt warm all over at the sound. She shook her hand as well, then left the two of them to their dinner and headed back into the kitchen.

"You are so dead," she said as she stalked toward her brother, who was laughing hysterically. "Do you want to be buried or cremated?"

"Oh my God, you should have seen your face," Joey managed to spit out between bursts of laughter. He motioned at Greg, one of their employees. "You can go home, man. See you tomorrow."

"I'd think you'd want a witness to what I'm planning to do to you," Lana said. She looked at Greg, who was laughing as well, but at least he had the decency to stop when he realized she could easily turn her anger toward him. She nodded when he clocked out and practically ran through the back door.

❖

"She was so flirting with you," Gail said with a grin before taking a bite.

"She was not," Court replied, but she couldn't stop grinning for some reason. Lana was hot, there was no doubt about it. Dark hair, dark eyes, beautiful bone structure in her cheeks and jaw. And the voice? Sexy as all hell. Court shook her head and grabbed a slice of her own.

"You were just thinking about her."

"Stop." Court glanced over her shoulder and saw Lana watching them from the kitchen. What if she had been flirting? It wouldn't necessarily be a bad thing, would it? She sighed because it really didn't matter one way or the other. Between her work at the Realtor's office, hockey practice and games, not to mention the travel for road games, there wasn't much time left over for *anything*, let alone a relationship.

"Court, listen to me," Gail said. She set her slice down and wiped her hands on a napkin before turning her attention to her. Court knew this meant she was being serious, and she'd better listen if she knew what was good for her. Gail was the big sister she never had. "You can't live your life without companionship. As far as I know, you never even have sex."

Court almost choked on the bite of pizza she was trying to swallow. She got it to go down without any lasting damage, then took a healthy swig of her beer before leaning back in her seat.

"Speaking of companionship, where's your husband tonight?" Court asked. "He'd tell you to back off and leave me alone."

"He's home with the kids." Gail batted her eyes. "Too bad for you."

"I have sex, okay?" Court whispered as she leaned forward. "Not that it's any of your business."

"By yourself doesn't count."

"Jesus." Court hung her head. She felt her cheeks flush, and she couldn't remember the last time she'd been embarrassed enough to blush. After a moment she met Gail's eyes again. "Not by myself. You can be such an ass sometimes."

"Wait, you never masturbate?" Gail looked shocked, and Court was blushing again just as Lana returned to the table.

"How is everything, ladies?" she asked. Court hoped to God she hadn't heard any of their conversation. Her smile gave away nothing.

"Fine," Court said, perhaps a little too quickly. Lana's head tilted to the side. "Everything is great."

"Good." Lana stood there a moment longer. "Can I get you anything else?"

"Actually," Gail said as she was looking back and forth between Lana and Court, and Court knew exactly what was coming.

"Gail, don't," she said, trying to sound threatening.

"I was wondering if you could settle a bet between us," Gail said. Court fought the urge to slide out of the booth and under the table. She was going to kill Gail someday.

"Okay," Lana said, sounding intrigued and hesitant at the same time. "If I can."

Court started to stand up, seriously considering leaving, but Gail kicked her in the shin under the table. She managed to not yell out in pain, but Gail had achieved her goal. Court wouldn't be getting up any time soon.

"I say you were flirting with her earlier," Gail said, pointing a finger at Court. Court refused to look at Lana. This was so not cool. "She insists you weren't."

"Oh," Lana said. She was silent for a few seconds, and Court was unable to keep from looking up at her any longer.

She placed a hand firmly on Court's shoulder and leaned down to speak into her ear. "Maybe I wasn't doing it right? I'll be sure to make it more obvious next time."

Lana winked at her and walked away then, and Court felt as though she were frozen in place. The pulse was pounding in her ears, but she saw Gail speaking to her, even though she wasn't able to hear her.

"What?" Court asked when her heart finally slowed down.

"What did she say?" Gail asked, sounding impatient.

"She said she wasn't." Court lied before shoving more food in her mouth. Yeah, Gail had been the impetus, but Court didn't want to share just yet. It was almost as if she could still hear Lana's voice in her ear, and she could definitely still smell the peppermint that had been on her breath.

"You are such a liar," Gail said. "You forget I know you so well."

"Sometimes, I would seriously like to forget it," Court said. Gail looked so shocked, Court simply smiled. It wasn't often she could put Gail in her place.

CHAPTER THREE

Lana walked into the Realtor's office the next afternoon, thankful she was on time since Joey hadn't really wanted to let her have time off to do it in the first place. They were still working on what the best work schedule for her would be, so she didn't have times set in stone where she had to be there. She had the newspaper with the listing she was interested in rolled up in her hand as she walked up to the woman sitting at the front desk of the office.

"Can I help you?" she asked, her voice just this side of being too cheery for Lana.

"I have an appointment with Bill Crawford," Lana said.

"Oh, Mr. Crawford is running late this afternoon," the receptionist told her, sounding genuinely apologetic. "He isn't sure what time he'll make it in, but he's set you up with one of his agents if that's all right with you."

"Okay," Lana said, not really happy about it since she'd spent so much time on the phone with Bill the day before, but she took a calming breath. She didn't like when things didn't go the way she'd planned.

"If you'll follow me, I'll take you to Ms. Abbott's office."

Lana nodded and let her lead the way. The office as a whole was nice, albeit small, and Lana assumed there were only a couple of agents working with Bill Crawford. The woman in front of her stopped so abruptly, Lana almost plowed her over.

"Ms. Abbott, your appointment is here," she said.

Lana gave herself a quick once-over, making sure there were no wrinkles in her blouse or her slacks, although she wasn't quite sure why she felt the need to impress the real estate agent. The receptionist stepped aside and motioned her in, and Lana walked past her. When she looked at the woman behind the desk, she froze, not quite sure what to do.

"Hello, Courtney Court," she managed after a moment, hoping no one had noticed her slight hesitation. She relaxed a bit when Court graced her with a big smile. "But the receptionist said I was meeting with Ms. Abbott. Please don't tell me your name isn't Courtney Court. To be honest it's kind of grown on me."

"Please, have a seat," Court said as she reached out a hand. Lana took it briefly, but she had a hard time letting go of it for some reason. "Sorry to disappoint you, but I am Courtney Abbott. You can call me Court."

"Okay, Court it is." Lana sat and crossed her legs.

"So, Bill tells me you're looking for a six-month lease, is that right?" Court asked as she was sifting through the papers she had in front of her.

"Yes, I'll be going back to Chicago in a few months." It sounded as though Bill had filled her in on what they'd talked about, so Lana felt better about being handed off. And the fact Court was surely nicer to look at than Bill would have been didn't hurt matters either.

"Oh, okay," Court said, sounding disappointed, though

Lana simply smiled. The thought she might be saddened by the news of her leaving left a warm feeling in her chest.

"I'm interested in this one," Lana said, holding the newspaper out to her with the ad circled in bold black lines. She watched Court as she read the ad, then began typing something into the computer. God, she was gorgeous. Lana shook her head. She wasn't here looking for anything. She was here to help out her family while her father recovered from his heart attack. But damn, a fling with Courtney Abbott would be something to remember, she was sure. "I know it's listed for sale, but I was hoping they might be willing to do a lease."

"Are you free to go take a look at it now?" Court asked when she finally looked at her again.

"Sure," Lana said, nodding.

"Let me call the listing agent and let him know, then we can head on over there." Court picked up the phone on her desk and talked to Lana as she was dialing. "I'm pretty sure these people really are more interested in selling than leasing, but we might be able to work something out. It's probably best to look at it first before I even bring it up to them, though. You might not even like it."

Lana nodded again, thinking she was pretty sure she would like it, unless the inside was a complete and total mess. She'd driven by the house yesterday. It was a cute little ranch and was within walking distance of the school, which would be great for Eric. An added bonus was it was also fairly close to the pizzeria. And it wasn't her parents' house, so there was that.

"Okay, we're all set," Court said as she stood and grabbed her jacket. She smiled at Lana again, and Lana thought she just might melt right there on Court's office floor.

They rode to the house in silence, although Court kept looking at her as if she wanted to say something. Lana didn't really think she was so intimidating, but she was kind of enjoying the effect she seemed to be having on Court. When they arrived, Lana followed Court on a paved path leading to the front door. It was October, so there weren't a lot of flowers still around, but she could see the pathway was flanked with many plants that would no doubt die under her care once spring arrived. Oh well, plenty of time to worry about killing flowers later.

Court got the key out of the lock box and opened the door, motioning for Lana to walk in ahead of her. Lana stopped just inside the doorway and took it all in. The house was obviously well cared for. A nice hardwood floor led from the front door to the kitchen, which was straight ahead of them. A living room to the right, and a hallway leading to what Lana assumed was the master suite. A hall to the left led to the second bedroom and bath. Eric would like being on the opposite end of the house.

"Shall we look around?" Court asked, walking past her and into the kitchen.

Seeing the kitchen almost made Lana wish she knew how to cook. Almost. She could make lasagna, but not much else that didn't come out of a box or a can. The stainless steel appliances were fantastic, and the island situated between the stove and the small kitchen table was almost big enough to use as a dining table itself.

She followed Court down the hallway to the second bedroom, and nodded as she stood in the middle of the room, picturing Eric there. Since the owners were looking to sell, Lana was a little surprised to find the house fully furnished. She hoped the furniture was going to stay, because otherwise they might be sleeping on air mattresses for the next few months.

"This is perfect," she said, not realizing she'd spoken out loud.

"For an office? Because the master is at the other end of the house," Court said.

"No, for my son," Lana said, and she thought she saw a hint of panic wash over Court's features. For some reason, the notion of Court not liking kids worried her, though logically she knew it didn't matter in the grand scheme of things.

"You have a son?"

"I do. Is that a problem?"

"No, of course not," Court said as she looked down at the sheet she held in her hand and scratched her neck. "Nope, kids are great."

"As long as they're someone else's?" Lana walked toward her and ducked her head to try to look at Court's face.

"Something like that." Court chuckled. "Is there a husband too?"

"No, there isn't." Lana thought back to the night before. "Do you really think I would have been flirting with you if I were married?"

"It's not unheard of."

"I've never been married." Lana walked out of the room and headed for the master suite. Without looking to make sure Court was following, she tossed over her shoulder, "Maybe someday I'll tell you all about it."

❖

Tell me about it? Lord, I don't think I want to know.
Court didn't have a problem with bi-women, but she sure

as hell didn't want to hear about what they did with guys. She was definitely not into that much sharing.

She hurried to the other end of the house to catch up with Lana. She was waiting outside the double doors, which were closed. Court reached around her and opened them, revealing a short hall leading to the sleeping area on the right, and the master bath on the left.

"This is a great bathroom," Lana said with a nod as she ran her hand along the marble countertop. "Oh. My. God." Lana stopped and simply stared at the shower in front of her. There were two showerheads, one on each side, and a clear glass door, twice the size of any conventional shower door. "This has got to be big enough for four people."

Four? Now Court was sure she didn't want to hear about what Lana had alluded to a few minutes before. But seriously, would she do that with a child in the house?

"Of course, I'd never have more than one other person in there with me," Lana said with a smirk and a wink, and Court wondered if she could read her mind. "You should see your face."

Court looked at herself in the huge mirror behind the sinks and took a step backward. She looked horrified by what she'd been thinking, and she couldn't help but laugh at herself.

"I'm sorry," Court said, shaking her head.

"Don't be. It's kind of cute."

More flirting? Really? Court was so far removed from the last time she'd flirted, she wasn't sure she even remembered how to do it.

"Okay, well, what do you think of the house?" Court asked, deciding a change of subject was a good idea. "I can call the listing agent and see about a lease if it's what you want."

"Six months for sure, and maybe a month-to-month for

one or two more, if they'd be willing to do it," Lana said. "If not, I suppose I could go back to my parents' for the last month or so until school is done for the year."

"You're here from Chicago, right?" Court asked, remembering her mentioning it earlier.

"Yes, I'm subletting my apartment there through May, so I can't go back until at least then."

"Can I ask why you're here?" Court began walking back toward the front door. "Unless I'm being too personal. I'm sorry. It's none of my business."

"I don't mind." Lana shrugged as they got into Court's car to head back to her office. "I grew up here. When I left for college, I just never came back. I've been in Chicago ever since, but my father had a heart attack about a week ago, and my brother asked me to come home to help with things while he recovers. Which is why I'm working at the pizzeria with him."

"What do you do in Chicago?"

"I'm second violin in the orchestra."

"Wow," Court said, wondering if she should be impressed, and figuring she probably should be. "How long have you been doing that?"

"Seems like forever. They were nice enough to grant me a leave of absence so I could be here for my family."

"That's great."

Court saw Lana look at her out of the corner of her eye, but she didn't want to look back at her. She didn't want to let on she knew nothing about orchestras. To Court, it had always been something for people with a lot of money, and she'd never been included in those groups.

"Have dinner with me tonight," Lana said.

"I can't," Court told her, feeling more disappointed than she should. "I have a game tonight."

"A game?" Lana was obviously confused, and Court tried to hide her smile. "It's too late in the season for softball so, basketball?"

"Ice hockey."

"No shit," Lana said, sounding happy at the admission. "You play for the Warriors?"

"I do." Court pulled into her parking spot outside of the real estate office and turned off the engine. She turned in her seat to face Lana. "But they haven't existed very long, so if you've been in Chicago since college, how do you know about the women's ice hockey team here in Kingsville?"

"Ever heard of something called the internet?" There was that smirk again, and Court was starting to like it.

"You know, I think I might have." Court nodded, enjoying their easy banter.

"What time does it start? I might have to bring Eric to a game."

"Seven tonight." Court got out of the car and waited for Lana to join her. "I can leave tickets for you if you want to come. Eric is your son? He likes hockey?"

"Please, Eric loves hockey." Lana laughed and bumped Court with her shoulder. "He lives and breathes Blackhawks hockey. He started playing when he was ten, and yes, he's my son."

"What position?" Court finally relaxed since they were now onto a subject she knew a lot about.

"Center."

"Me too. You should definitely bring him to the game." Court held the door open for Lana to go ahead of her into the reception area. "Should I leave tickets for tonight?"

"Yeah, if it's not too much trouble."

"Not at all."

"Court, Gail called, wants you to call her back," said Rikki, the office receptionist.

"Thanks, Rikki," she said as they disappeared into her office.

"Gail?" Lana asked. "The woman you were with last night?"

"She's our coach," Court answered with a nod. "Bill, the guy you were supposed to meet with this morning, is her husband."

"So, not a girlfriend then?" Lana asked with a smile. Court felt her cheeks flush, and she looked down at the paper on the desk in front of her. She shook her head. "Good to know. Is there a girlfriend somewhere?"

"No," Court answered.

"What's wrong with you?"

Court whipped her head up and saw the smirk again. The one telling her *Relax, I'm just teasing you.* She sat back in her chair and held her hands clasped in her lap as she met Lana's eyes.

"Depends on who you ask." It was cryptic, but it was meant to be, and was apparently having the desired effect. Lana leaned forward and looked at her eagerly.

"Do tell," she said.

"I have work to do," Court said, putting an end to the inquiry. She smiled at the look of frustration on Lana's face. "As much as I would love to spend the day talking with you, I have to call the agent who listed the house you want, and I have to call my coach back. How many tickets do you need for tonight?"

"Two," she said, but hesitated. "Unless you'll have dinner with me after the game. Then I'd need three so my mother would be there to take Eric home."

"I'll leave two," Court said. "I always have dinner with Bill and Gail after games."

"Oh. Okay. Maybe some other time, then." Lana stood and walked toward the door. She stopped and looked back at her. "You'll call me if the owners agree to the lease?"

"I will." When she was gone, Court took a deep breath. What the hell was wrong with her? A beautiful woman asked her out to dinner, *twice*, and she turned her down. It was for the best, though, because Lana was going to be leaving again in a few months. While it might be fun to spend some alone time with Lana Caruso, she wasn't really wired that way. Sure, a one-night stand was fine when she was going out to bars with her line mates, because it was the purpose of those particular excursions. Something told Court she wouldn't be satisfied with a fling where Lana was concerned. And besides, Lana had a kid. Not something Court needed—or wanted—in her life.

Still, there was something about Lana she couldn't quite put her finger on. She wasn't anything like the women she usually met, and she was intrigued, for better or worse.

Chapter Four

Lana put her arm through Eric's as they walked across the street toward the arena. She couldn't believe he was fifteen and taller than she was, and she was by no means short at five foot ten. There weren't a lot of people there, but it seemed to be a fairly decent-sized crowd. She pulled Eric toward the will-call window to pick up the tickets Court said she'd leave for them.

"Mom," Eric said. "I can't believe you're bringing me to a *women's* hockey game."

"I know damn well you aren't a chauvinist, so tell me why you're acting like this. As I recall, it was the women in the Olympics who drew you in." She knew it was more or less because the women were more successful than the men at the Olympic level, but still. Lana turned away from him to tell the woman at the window her name. A few seconds later, tickets in hand, they were entering the arena. "You think women can't play hockey?"

"Mom," he said, his voice taking on the whining quality she was really beginning to dislike. He looked around in case there was anyone there he might know, which was silly, really, because he'd just transferred to the local school two days earlier. "You know that's not it."

"Then what is it?" Lana led him to their seats and they sat down. The arena was smaller than she'd expected and reminded her of the rinks Eric played in. The seats were metal benches, and the entire arena probably couldn't hold more than three thousand people.

"It's just a different kind of game is all," he said with a shrug as he looked around at the people. "Less physical. Nobody fights or anything."

"Eric, even the men don't play as physical in the Olympics." Lana turned her attention to the ice as the Warriors skated out for the start of the game. She'd hoped to arrive before warm-ups, but Eric had been finishing up his homework. She smiled when she saw a player with the name *Abbott* on her back. Number eight, which just happened to be Eric's number. "Just give it a chance, all right?"

"Okay." He sighed and watched the women skating. "Which one of them gave you the tickets?"

"Number eight," Lana said.

"No way." He was much more interested then, even though he tried to hide it.

"Yep," she answered. "Courtney Abbott. Apparently, she's the captain since she has that big C on her left shoulder."

"Courtney Abbott?" he asked, whipping his head around to look at her. "Are you serious?"

"You know who she is?" Lana was surprised, but she never took her eyes off Court.

"Yeah, and you should too," he told her. "She scored a hat trick in the gold medal game at the last Olympics. Jeez, Mom, you could have told me it was her."

"I didn't realize."

"You're going to introduce me after the game, right?" he

asked, but he was now concentrating on the ice too, as they were about to drop the puck to start the game.

"If she has time, I will," Lana promised, wondering how she hadn't known who Court was. Now that she'd been reminded, Court had been all Eric talked about for days after the USA won the gold medal almost four years ago.

They were seated a couple of rows behind the team benches, and when Court came off the ice after her first shift, she sat down and then turned her head and looked right at them. Lana gave her a little wave and then noticed Eric smiling at Court. She elbowed him in the ribs good-naturedly.

Midway through the first period, the Warriors were changing lines on the fly, and Court got tripped as she was coming off the bench. Everyone in the arena got to their feet as the whistle blew. A man Lana assumed was the trainer came out on the ice to check Court, but she got up on her own. One of her teammates held on to her jersey because it looked like Court wanted to go after someone, and Lana didn't blame her.

"Why aren't they calling a penalty?" she asked Eric.

"Because it was her own teammate who tripped her," he answered, pointing to a woman at the end of the bench who was laughing, but no one else was joining in. In fact, everyone else on the bench seemed to be inching away from her. "Number twelve. Hilton."

Lana watched as Gail went to Hilton, grabbed the back of her jersey and pulled on it hard, then leaned down and said something in her ear. Hilton stopped laughing almost immediately, and then Gail shoved her forward as she released her jersey and walked away once again.

At least Court didn't appear to be hurt, which was a relief. Everyone settled back in their seats as they got ready to start play again.

❖

"If I were you, Abbott, I'd be teaching the rookie a lesson," the center from the other team said to her as they both leaned in for the puck drop. They'd been teammates on the Olympic squad, and they'd become friends over the course of the time they'd played together.

Court just shook her head, not wanting to let anything but the impending faceoff occupy her thoughts. Her concentration was legendary, and she wasn't going to let someone like Hilton take her off her game.

"She'll get what's coming to her," Savannah said. "Trust me on that."

Court took a deep breath and won the faceoff, passing the puck back to the defense as they skated up the ice. The puck got dumped in the zone, and Court raced after it, beating everyone to it behind the net. Her usual move was to pass it to the right, but she knew they were expecting it, so she passed left to Kelly. While the goaltender scrambled to get back into position, Kelly quickly passed it back to Court, who had moved to the opposite side of the net. Since everyone on the other team had readjusted their positions, she had a wide open net to shoot at, and she buried the puck in the back of the net.

The arena erupted in cheers—it didn't hold many people, but they certainly were loud—as the other Warriors on the ice skated over to congratulate her. The players on the bench were standing and whacking their sticks against the boards in their own version of cheering for her goal.

The first period ended in a one-one tie, and Gail gave them all a pep talk in the locker room between periods. Court noticed no one was sitting anywhere near Hilton, and Gail never even looked in her direction. When the pep talk was done, Gail motioned for Court to come to her office. The team didn't have a dedicated locker room, and the office was no different. It was shared with other coaches, so as a result, there was nothing personal on the desk or the walls. Court shut the door behind them and looked out the window, where Hilton was still being ignored by her teammates.

"I'm going to call the owner," Gail told her. "I won't put up with shit like this on my team. It's bad enough she ran you into the boards in practice, but to purposely trip you during a game? In the middle of a line change with no stoppage in play? Not acceptable."

"Why are you telling me and not her?" Court tried not to sound angry, but she wasn't sure she was pulling it off.

"I did tell her, Court, but I thought you should hear it too. If I have anything to say about it, she won't be suiting up for the Warriors again. And after the stunt she pulled, I wouldn't be surprised if nobody in this league wanted her."

"That would be a shame," Court said, shaking her head. "Because I know a few people on this team who would love to introduce her to karma."

"Get this team fired up, because I want to win a championship again this year." Gail opened the door and motioned her out. Court wasn't surprised Gail ignored her last comment. During the games, she was "coach" Gail, and not "friend" Gail.

She went and sat by her locker and used a towel to wipe the sweat from her face. As she tossed the towel back into the locker, she felt a hand on her shoulder. She turned her head and saw Hilton standing behind her.

"I'm sorry," she said, but it didn't seem sincere to Court. No doubt she was only apologizing to try to get Court on her side, and to hopefully stay with the team. "It was an accident."

Court chuckled. "I might have believed you if you hadn't

thrown the last part in." Court stood and slammed the locker door shut. When she turned to face Hilton, she saw Savannah and Kelly heading toward them, but she put a hand up to stop them. "You and I both know it was no accident, so I suggest you keep your head up and stay the hell away from me. Whatever happens after the game is all on you."

She hadn't meant it as a threat, but realized it no doubt sounded like one. She'd simply been referring to the fact Gail was going to be calling the owner about what happened. It was obvious Hilton had taken it as a threat, though, because she turned away and stalked back to her own locker without another word.

The game was almost over and they were ahead three-two when Gail sent Hilton out for her only shift since the first period. Hilton almost had a breakaway, but she got caught with her head down in the neutral zone and was flattened by a vicious open ice check. She was down, and she wasn't moving. At all. Court was the first one over the boards and held her arm out for the trainer, who wasn't wearing skates.

She and Hilton pretty much hated each other, but for now they were on the same team, and Court would never turn her back on an injured teammate. She guided the trainer to Hilton and she stood there watching as he checked her out. The rest of the team stayed on the bench, and Court felt her anger rising. They should all be out there with her. Savannah could obviously tell she was pissed off, because she skated out and motioned for the rest of them to follow.

When Hilton finally got to her feet with the help of Court and the trainer, players on both teams hit their sticks on the ice, and the people in the stands cheered. Hilton gripped Court's jersey tightly until they got to the edge of the ice, then she let go and met Court's eyes.

"Thank you," she said quietly.

Court nodded and skated away, knowing the trainer could handle getting her into the locker room on his own. She went back to the bench and sat, and Gail walked behind her, giving her a squeeze on the shoulder.

They won the game three-two, and Court looked up to where Lana and her son were sitting. She didn't know what she'd been expecting, but Eric was older than she'd thought he'd be. Lana held a finger up to him and started to walk down the steps to the bench.

"My son wants to meet you. Is that all right?" Lana asked. Court nodded and Lana waved him down. "Great game, by the way. Is Hilton going to be all right?"

"I don't know," Court answered as she removed her helmet and gloves. She kind of wanted to get back to the locker room to find out, but she also wanted to stand there talking to Lana. She was getting under Court's skin, and she wasn't sure why. "She was out cold for a few seconds, so I'm sure they've already taken her to the hospital."

"Hi," Eric said when he finally got to them. He looked nervous, but Court had no idea why he would be. "I'm Eric."

"Court," she said with a smile. She shook his hand and glanced at Lana, who was beaming. Seeing them standing side by side, there was no doubt he was her son. He had the same dark hair and brown eyes, and the same high cheekbones. "It's nice to meet you, Eric."

"I can't believe I'm really meeting Courtney Abbott," he said, shifting his weight from one foot to the other. "You were so awesome in the Olympics."

"Thank you," she said with a nod. "It was a pretty cool experience. Your mom tells me you play hockey too."

"Yep, same position as you, and the same number too," he said, but then his smile faded, and he shrugged. "At least it was my number in Chicago."

"I'm sure you'll find a team here to play with, and you can usually pick your number, as long as nobody else on the team has it," Court told him.

"We should let you go," Lana said with a hand to Court's forearm.

"Okay," she answered, feeling the disappointment. She really wanted to get to know Lana better, but figured asking her out with her son there might not be the best idea. She looked at Eric. "It really was good to meet you. I'm sure I'll see you again sometime."

Chapter Five

L ana drove Eric to school the next morning, and when she
returned, her mother was just preparing to leave for the
hospital to see her father. Lana loved her parents dearly but
had never really been close with either of them. They'd started
their family later in life, so they'd been in their late fifties
when Lana graduated high school, and Joey was three years
younger than Lana. Her parents had grown up in a different
time, and they just didn't understand Lana's love of classical
music. But what they really didn't understand was when she'd
come out to them in her senior year of high school.

They accepted her, but they weren't thrilled about her
sexuality. As a result, they rarely spoke about it, but they'd
hoped the "phase" had ended when she announced she was
pregnant shortly after graduating college. She tried her best
to explain she wanted a baby, and her best friend, a gay man,
offered to help. They really couldn't fathom the concept of
artificial insemination.

"How is Dad?" she asked as she set her keys on the table
just inside the front door.

"The doctors say he's improving." It was as much of

a response as Lana could hope for. Her mother had gained weight in the years since Lana had left for college. She really needed to come home to visit more often. "You could go by and see him, you know."

"I know, Mom," she said, closing her eyes and trying to stave off a headache. "I will, but helping Joey at Caruso's is almost a full-time job."

"You weren't there last night." It was an accusation, and Lana did her best to ignore the implied complaint.

"No, I wasn't. I wanted to take Eric to see a hockey game. He isn't happy about having to leave his home and all of his friends back in Chicago." Lana sat at the kitchen table her parents had owned since before she was born. "So if I can do anything to make his life more enjoyable while we're here, then I'm going to do it."

Her mother nodded but said nothing, her lips pursed.

"What?" Lana asked, not bothering to hide her irritation.

"I didn't say anything."

"But you want to," Lana said. "So just say it."

"I just don't understand why you let him play hockey. Why do you encourage him?" Her mother sighed and buttoned up her coat. "It's a waste of time if you ask me. He'll never go anywhere with it, and he'll probably end up getting hurt."

"He's really good, Mom," Lana said. "There are junior teams in our area already scouting him. You should see him play sometime, and I know you'd change your mind."

"How can I see him play when you live in Chicago?"

And there it was. This was always what it came down to, which was why Lana didn't visit more often—hardly at all, really. And why she knew she wouldn't be able to live in this house until she and Eric returned to Chicago at the end of the school year. She got to her feet and poured herself a cup of coffee. She had a feeling she was going to need the caffeine today.

"Did Kingsville finally get an orchestra?" She knew her voice was dripping with sarcasm, but she couldn't find the energy to care.

"You know the answer to that."

"Until they do, I'll be staying in Chicago."

"What about Philadelphia or New York?" her mother asked. "Or Allentown?"

"You're kidding, right?" Lana walked back to the table and sat as she stared at her mother, incredulous. "Chicago has one of the top symphony orchestras in the world, and you want me to come to Allentown? New York and Philadelphia are amongst the best also, but they're both at least an hour and a half from here, and only if there's no traffic, which we both know never happens."

"I'm not saying you'd have to live *here*," her mother said, her tone indicating her own frustration. "But they'd both be a hell of a lot closer than Chicago."

Her mother turned on her heel and left the house without giving Lana an opportunity to answer. Lana just sat there staring at the front door long after she'd left, wondering why her mother would even want to have her live close by. Her parents didn't approve of her being a lesbian, so she could only imagine how well it would go over if she ever met a woman she wanted to make a life with.

The only thing she could figure was it had to be a cultural thing. Both sets of Lana's grandparents had moved to the United States from Italy with *their* parents. Probably on the same damn boat, for all Lana knew. Family always lived close by, for as long as Lana could remember. She'd always found it stifling, but apparently Joey enjoyed it, because he still lived at home.

Lana shuddered at the thought. She really hoped the owners of the house she looked at were willing to lease it to her.

❖

Court didn't want to, but Gail insisted the entire team go to visit Jen Hilton in the hospital. She'd suffered a pretty bad concussion because of the hit she'd taken, but she was expected to be okay and be able to play again in a few weeks. She walked into the room carrying a small flower arrangement she'd picked up at the hospital gift shop, mostly as an afterthought because it just felt wrong to go in empty-handed.

"Jesus Christ," Hilton muttered when Court came in and walked to her bed. "What the hell is going on? I think half the team has been here already this morning. I have to admit you were the last one I thought would show up, though."

"Just wanted to let you know I'm thinking about you," Court said, having to turn away and set the flowers on the bedside table so Hilton couldn't see the grimace she was unable to keep off her face. It wasn't that Court was happy she got hurt, it was simply the idea of having to do this after Hilton intentionally tripped her during a game that really irked her.

"Why?"

"Excuse me?" Court looked at her.

"Why are you thinking about me?" Hilton watched her carefully, and Court fought to keep a straight face. "You don't even like me."

"Well, you did kind of bring it on yourself, didn't you?" Court asked as she pulled a chair closer to the bed and sat. "We don't have to like each other when we're away from the rink. But when we're playing, or even practicing for that matter, we need to work together. We're a team, Hilton. When you fail, so do the rest of us."

"I won't fail," she said. "I've never failed at anything."

"You did last night." Court watched as Hilton opened her mouth to say something, but then turned her head away. "You tripped me, and then you laughed about it. And then someone from the other team decided to teach you a lesson."

"Teach me a lesson for what? For tripping you? Isn't that something you or one of the other Warriors should do?" Hilton laughed and shook her head slowly. "You need people from other teams to fight for you?"

"What happened had nothing to do with me," Court told her. She was afraid of this. Hilton was far too confident in her own abilities as a playmaker. As far as Hilton was concerned, there wasn't anything anybody could possibly teach her about the game. "It happened because you were skating through the neutral zone with your head down. When you do that, you run the risk of getting your bell rung."

"No, it happened because somebody took a cheap shot at me."

"Have you ever played a physical game before? Maybe you've played in leagues where the physical aspect has been taken out?" Court shook her head. "It was a clean hit. If you'd had your head up, you would have seen it coming and been able to get out of the way. But you were so intent on getting up the ice and scoring, nothing else even penetrated your brain. Not even your teammates yelling at you to look up."

"I'm a better player than you've ever been."

Court sighed. This was going about as well as she'd told Gail it would. If she'd known this would be her path, she would have declined when offered the captaincy of the team. It would be so easy to just get up and leave the room, but walking away from something only because it was difficult wasn't who she was. It never had been. Her father had always told her anything worth having was worth fighting for.

"Maybe you are," Court conceded with a shrug. "Then again, maybe you aren't. I can tell you one thing for sure, though. If you keep this attitude, and continue to play the way you did last night, no one will ever know whether you're better than me or not, because concussions will force you to retire before you're thirty."

"Fuck you." Hilton waved toward the door, obviously dismissing her, but Court refused to move. "Leave. Now."

They both stared at each other, and after a few moments, Court began to smile. This was so insanely stupid. She'd dealt with many players over the years who thought they were going to be the ones who changed the game. None of them ever did, and in fact, quickly came back down to earth after they'd played a few games and realized it wasn't going to be as easy for them as it had been in high school, or wherever else they'd played before. This time it wasn't going to be so easy.

"What the hell are you smiling at?" Hilton asked.

"Nothing," Court said with a shake of her head.

"You're a lesbian," Hilton said, and Court laughed. She couldn't help it.

"And you're a bigot, but I fail to see what either of those things have to do with playing hockey." Court got to her feet and stood next to the bed looking down at her. "Yes, I am a lesbian, but it isn't all I am. Just as I'm sure being a bigot isn't all you are. The sooner you can get past all of that, the sooner we can go back to being a unified team."

Court walked away without waiting for a response. She was fuming, but she knew it didn't show outwardly. When she got to the elevator she took a moment to try to calm herself. Court had never hated anyone in her life, but Jen Hilton was certainly doing her best to push her toward it now.

Chapter Six

"How'd it go?" Gail asked later the same afternoon as she stood in the doorway of Court's office.

"Just peachy," Court replied.

"That well, huh?"

"She's making me seriously rethink my philosophy of never hating anyone."

"Well, she won't be playing for a couple of weeks at least." Gail pushed off the doorframe and came to sit in the chair facing Court's desk. "Maybe before she even gets back to practice I can convince the brass to trade her."

"Hope springs eternal," Court said, allowing a slight grin at the thought. She leaned back in her chair and laced her fingers together behind her head. "What can I do for you?"

"Oh, I just stopped by to see Bill for a minute," Gail said. "I had a bit of time to kill before meeting a client who wants to see the house in Easton."

"Have you guys given any thought to what I mentioned yesterday?"

"Bill's working on the lease now." Gail leaned forward. "You like her, don't you?"

"Even if I did, it doesn't really matter much." Court sighed and turned her head to look out the window. "She only wants to lease because she's going back to Chicago at the end of the school year. Which leads to the second problem."

"Which is?"

"She has a kid."

"And?"

"Do you even know me?" Court looked at her as though Gail had lost her mind. She knew how Court felt about kids.

"Court, you're great with kids," Gail told her. "I don't know why you seem to have a mental block when it comes to anyone under seventeen."

"I just don't want them living with me."

"Nobody said you have to marry the woman, for God's sake," Gail said with a laugh. "Can't you date her for a while and see how things go?"

"No."

"Why not? You're the one who's always insisted you don't have time for anything serious, so why can't you just spend time with her while she's in town?"

"No." Court stared at her, wondering why she was being so rigid with this. Gail was right. She'd never had a relationship last more than three months, so what made Lana so different? She had a kid, that's what. She'd never dated anyone who had a kid.

"You are infuriating sometimes, do you know that?" Gail stood and took a couple steps toward the door.

"But you love me anyway." Court grinned.

"If I didn't, you wouldn't have a job here," Gail answered with a grin of her own. She waved as she disappeared through the doorway. "Tell her the owners want to meet her, tonight, nine o'clock."

Court reached for her cell phone as soon as Gail was gone, but she held it in her hand, just staring at it. Would it be so bad to just see where things might lead between her and Lana? As long as she knew Lana was going to be leaving in a few months, what would be the harm? If they cozied up together, it would certainly make the winter months in the Poconos more bearable. She smiled and found Lana's number in her phone.

"Courtney Court," she said when she answered the call, causing Court to laugh. "You have a really nice laugh. Has anyone ever told you that before?"

"No, I don't think they have."

"What a shame, because it's true. Are you calling me with good news?"

"As a matter of fact, yes, I am," Court told her. "The people who own the house would like to meet with you tonight to sign the paperwork. Are you free?"

"What time?"

"Nine o'clock."

"Kind of late for a meeting, isn't it?" Lana asked, and Court waited as Lana sighed and sounded as though she sat down. "Should I be worried about them? They aren't serial killers or anything, are they?"

"No, I assure you they are not," Court said. "I'll be there too if it makes you feel any better."

"You know what? I think it might. What's their address?"

"I could pick you up," Court offered. If she was going to see where things went, why not start as soon as possible? "Or you could meet me at the real estate office. Or I could just give you the address."

"Why don't you pick me up at the pizzeria?"

"If you have to work, I can schedule this for another time," Court said, not even having considered she might have to work.

"If it was a weekend, I probably would, but Joey can handle things without me for tonight."

"I can be there at eight forty-five, if that works for you."

"Then I will see you tonight."

Lana ended the call and shoved the phone into her back pocket before heading to the kitchen to tell Joey he'd have to close on his own. She didn't care how much he bitched and moaned about it, she wasn't going to put off the possibility of having her own living space for another day.

"I'm leaving early tonight," she said as she pulled a pizza out of the oven and placed it on the counter to slice it.

"Usually you *ask* if you can leave early," he told her, trying to look serious. "You don't *tell* the boss you are."

"Maybe if you were the boss, I would have asked." She stuck her tongue out at him and he laughed.

"I've missed you, Lana," he said with a grin. "Why do you have to live so far away?"

"Seriously? Did Mom tell you to ask me that?"

"No," he answered before disappearing into the walk-in cooler to retrieve more cheese. "I just miss you. I think it would be great if you and Eric moved back here for good."

"Not going to happen, sorry, Joey," she said.

"Why are you leaving early tonight?" Lana was thankful he was in tune with her enough to know when he should change the subject.

"Remember the house I told you about?" she asked. He nodded his response. "I'm signing the paperwork tonight. And meeting the people who own it. Hopefully by the end of the weekend, Eric and I will be living in our own space."

"Mom won't be happy about this unexpected turn of events," he said, shaking his head.

"She'll just have to get over it," Lana replied with a shrug.

"She can't really have assumed we'd stay with them for the entire time we're here, could she?"

"She's Mom," he answered. "So, yeah."

"I'd go crazy living there," she told him. "I honestly don't know how you can do it."

He shrugged and wiped his hands on the towel he had in his apron pocket. He turned and leaned against the counter to face her.

"They don't charge me rent. I put all the money I earn into a bank account, and I know if I ever need to, I'll have plenty of money to make it on my own. Besides, they aren't getting any younger, you know. I help out around the house."

"Please tell me you have a girlfriend, at least. You aren't one of those guys who lives with his parents and has no social life, are you?"

"I've been seeing someone," he said. "It's still new, so I haven't said anything to Mom and Dad about her yet. Please don't tell them. I'm not ready for them to meet her."

"Your secret's safe with me," Lana assured him. She was happy he'd found someone. He'd always been a bit nerdy growing up, and hadn't had a lot of friends. He'd definitely grown into a nice looking guy, but she knew it couldn't help that he was still living at home at almost thirty-three years old.

"What about you?" he asked. "You have a girlfriend waiting for you back in Chicago?"

"No," she answered with a snort. "The women I meet are a little too high class for me. And when they find out I have a fifteen-year-old son, well, let's just say they tend to run pretty fast in the other direction. I need someone a little more down-to-earth, you know?"

"Someone who likes to chill after work instead of getting all dressed up and spending the night on the town?"

"Exactly," Lana answered, her mind going to Courtney Abbott. But then again, maybe not. She hadn't seemed thrilled when she found out about Eric. But she'd been warm and friendly when she'd introduced them the night before. "And someone who doesn't have a problem with my kid."

"If they have a problem with him, then they aren't worth it, sis," he said. "He's a good kid. You've done a good job raising him."

"Thank you," she said, not really accustomed to praise from her younger brother. They could still push each other's buttons, but she was glad to see he'd matured into a good man.

❖

Lana removed her apron and tossed it into the laundry bin when she saw Court walk through the door. She was putting her coat on as she leaned in and gave Joey a kiss on the cheek. He looked out into the dining room and saw Court before shaking his head.

"Looks to me like you have a hot date," he said, teasing.

"I wish," she muttered before she could stop the words. "She is hot, I'll agree with your assessment, but she's my real estate agent. Not a date."

"Too bad. But if you don't make it home tonight, I'll cover for you at breakfast." He winked at her and laughed as she ignored his remark and hustled out of the kitchen, ushering Court back through the doors and to the sidewalk.

"In a hurry?" Court asked her, looking amused.

"You have no idea," Lana answered with a shake of her head. She took a step back and looked at her for a moment. Her hair was wet, and Lana raised one eyebrow. "Just came from practice?"

"Yes, and I didn't want to smell like sweat."

"I'm sure I smell like pizza."

"Which is preferable to sweat, trust me."

Court opened the passenger side door for her, and Lana smiled at her. It had been a long time since another woman had opened a car door for her, and if Lana wasn't careful, she might actually begin to think this was a date.

CHAPTER SEVEN

W ho owns the house, and why are we meeting with them so late?" Lana asked as Court pulled into the driveway.

"Bill and Gail Crawford own the house," Court said as she cut the engine. She hadn't intended to tell her, and in fact, Gail had wanted to surprise her with it, but Court knew Lana wasn't the type to play games. She wasn't entirely sure how she knew it, she just did. "And we're meeting them so late because Gail probably only got home from practice about twenty minutes ago."

"You're sneaky," Lana said, but she was smiling, so Court relaxed. "I'll have to keep an eye on you."

"I hope you do," Court answered, but she looked away when she felt her face growing hot. Maybe she wasn't as out of practice as she thought she was where flirting was concerned.

"Trust me, it wouldn't be a hardship," Lana said, and Court opened her door to get out, knowing if they stayed there much longer, she might not let Lana out at all. Wouldn't Gail have fun with that? She waited on her side of the car for Lana, who placed a hand on her forearm when she walked up to her. "I'm sorry. Did I make you uncomfortable?"

"Not at all." Court hoped she wouldn't be struck down for lying. The fact was, Lana made her plenty uncomfortable. But only because she wanted to kiss her so badly. Court shook her head and motioned for Lana to go ahead of her along the path leading to the front door.

"Welcome, please come in," Gail said, opening the door before they were even close enough to think about knocking. Court rolled her eyes, knowing Gail had no doubt been watching out the window for them to pull into the driveway. Gail placed a hand on Lana's forearm. "You haven't met Bill yet, have you?"

"No, I've only spoken to him on the phone," Lana answered as she held a hand out to Bill.

"It's nice to finally meet you," Bill said as he gripped her hand briefly and gave her the megawatt smile Court was certain he thought made women's knees go weak. He was a handsome man with chiseled features and dark hair, so Court was sure his smile did have that effect, just not on her. "And I apologize for dumping you into Court's lap."

Lana glanced at Court and gave her a wink, and Court hurriedly removed her coat and handed it to Gail to cover her embarrassment at his words.

"It wasn't much of a hardship," Lana told him. Gail took her coat as well, and then they all headed for the kitchen.

"Boys, come say hello to Aunt Court, and then off to bed," Bill said as they walked past the living room.

Court smiled as the two boys, Bill Jr. and Carl, ran to her and spoke over each other in an attempt to get her attention. She crouched down so she could look them in the eye.

"Are you two behaving yourselves?" she asked them. When Carl started to answer, Billy interrupted.

"I am, but he's been bad," he said, pointing to his younger brother.

"Have not," Carl responded, giving Billy a punch in the arm. He seemed to notice Lana for the first time and was looking up at her when he leaned closer to Court. Court crouched lower so she was closer to his size. He pointed up at Lana and whispered, "Who is she?"

"This is Lana," Court said before making the introductions.

"She's pretty," Carl said with a nod. Court wasn't really sure how to respond, and thankfully, Lana saved her from what could have been an awkward moment.

"Aren't you sweet?" Lana said before placing a hand on Court's shoulder. "You're awfully handsome yourself, Carl."

Carl giggled and ran down the hall to his bedroom. Court knew exactly how he felt. Billy shook Lana's hand and glanced down the hall.

"Nice to meet you," he said, his smile looking much like his father's. "My brother's stupid."

"Billy," Gail said in a stern voice. He looked at his feet. Strangely, Court knew exactly how he felt too. "Your brother is young, he is not stupid. Say good night."

"Good night," he said without looking up again. He too disappeared down the hall to his own room.

"They're so cute," Lana said once they were all seated around the kitchen table. "How old are they?"

"Six and eight," Bill answered with a shake of his head. "They're definitely a handful."

"I remember that age," Lana told them. "My son is fifteen going on thirty. Sometimes I miss him being eight. But most of the time I thank God he isn't."

"I'm dreading the teenage years myself," Gail said.

"I was too, but it hasn't been bad yet. Eric is a good kid."

"You have the lease?" Court asked, tired of talking about kids. Her younger sister, Lori, had a boy and a girl, and Court loved babysitting for her when she could, but she was always thankful when Lori returned home and she could hand them back off.

"Nice segue, Court." Bill chuckled as he opened a file folder and pulled out the lease. He handed it to Lana so she could look it over. "It's pretty straightforward. Six months, with an option to go month-to-month after. The furniture in the house can stay if you want, and we would just need first and last month's rent, and you'll be ready to move in."

"Can I ask why you moved out of the house?" Lana asked.

"Well, we decided since the boys are getting older, it might be a good idea for them to have their own rooms," Gail said. "We outgrew it, basically."

Lana nodded and signed everything after she'd read the whole thing. Bill handed her the key after she wrote them a check.

"I can't tell you how grateful I am to have this house," she said. "My brother still lives at home, but I don't think I could stay there for the entire school year. I love my parents, don't get me wrong. I just haven't spent this much time with my mother since I left for college."

"I get it, trust me." Gail laughed, but Court knew she was close with her parents. "Court says you're here to help out your family while your father is recovering from a heart attack?"

"Yeah, they're saying it will be a few months before he'll be able to get back to the pizzeria, so I'm mostly helping Joey at the restaurant."

"I'm sorry to hear about your father," Bill said. "But I'm curious as to why you're planning to stay through the school year. Of course, I'm assuming it won't take eight months for him to recover."

"Eric didn't want to come here at all, but it wasn't an option."

"What about his father?" Bill asked.

Court wanted to excuse herself, but this was something she was at least mildly curious about as well. She'd been wondering if Lana was actually a lesbian, or if she was bisexual. Not that it mattered, since nothing was going to happen between them, right? But damn it, Court really wanted it to.

"He was my best friend in college," Lana said, looking as though she weren't entirely comfortable sharing this story. "We were both gay, and I wanted a child. He offered to help. Unfortunately, he passed away when Eric was nine. So, father not an option either."

"I'm sorry," Bill said.

"Thank you. It was hard on Eric for a while, but we've finally moved beyond it." Lana sighed and Court thought she physically forced herself to stop thinking about him and smiled as she looked at all of them. "Anyway, Eric compromised with me. He'd come willingly if I promised not to make him move in the middle of the school year. He had a friend who did that, and he was miserable, so he wanted to make sure he wasn't put in the same type of situation, especially since this is his first year in high school."

"Wow, that's awfully mature of him," Gail said with a pointed look at Court, which Court ignored. She knew what Gail was trying to do. She was no doubt assuming if Court could think of Eric as a young man instead of a child, maybe she could get past the barrier of not wanting to get involved with Lana.

"Look at the time," Court said as she glanced at the clock on the stove. "We should probably get going."

"It's not even ten," Gail said, but Court looked at her with what she hoped was a stern face. It apparently worked because Gail backed off. "But you're right. Bill has an appointment first thing in the morning."

"Thank you for everything," Lana said as they put on their

coats at the front door. "I promise I'll take good care of your house."

"Is there any chance you'll end up staying here permanently?" Bill asked.

"No," Lana answered with a shake of her head. No hesitation. Court felt a little disappointment at her quick response. "No, there's not."

Chapter Eight

They didn't speak much after they left Bill and Gail's, but Court needed to know where she was dropping her off. She thought about inviting Lana to her house for a drink, but then realized it might not be such a good idea.

"Am I taking you home, or back to the pizza place?" Court asked.

"You can take me home anytime," Lana replied. Court glanced at her and saw she was smiling. She couldn't help but smile back.

"Do you flirt with everyone?" Court asked.

"No, I don't," she said. "But it's really easy with you. And you're cute when you blush."

"Thanks, I think." Court laughed in spite of herself.

"I'm sorry. I'll stop if you want me to."

"I never said I didn't like it." Court stole another glance at her and saw she was looking down at her hands. "Actually, I do. Like it, I mean."

"Good to know." Lana sighed. "When's your next game?"

"Next home game isn't until next Wednesday. We play a couple of games on the road this weekend, though. One down near Philly and the other out by Pittsburgh."

"How far do you guys travel? And *how* do you travel?"

"The team has a bus, and believe it or not, we go as far west as Chicago."

"I bet that's fun by bus," Lana said. "But I had no idea the Wolves were in the same league as Kingsville. I'm sure I would if I kept up with it, but unfortunately, the orchestra plays mostly at night, so I don't have much time to go to hockey games. Except for Eric's, of course."

"The bus ride can be tedious, but it's not so bad when everyone gets along," Court said, her mind going back to Jen Hilton. Road trips weren't something she was looking forward to this season with her on the team.

"But you don't all get along, do you?"

"We have in the past." Court shrugged as she turned onto her own street, only then realizing she wasn't even thinking about where she was going. "But no, at the moment we don't. I'm sorry. I should have asked where to drop you off."

"You did. I thought we decided you could take me home." Lana sounded amused. "Your home will do."

Court felt her heart rate quicken, and she wondered if this was a good idea. Then she realized it was ridiculous to feel nervous about being alone with Lana. They were both adults. They could sit in her living room and have a glass of wine without anything happening between them, couldn't they? She took in a deep breath and pulled into her driveway.

"This is it," she said as she shut off the car.

"Nice neighborhood."

They both sat in silence for a few moments, and Court heard Lana chuckle. She turned her head and met her eyes.

"Are we going to sit out here all night, or should we go inside?" Lana asked.

Without a word, Court got out of the car and went to her front door, Lana right behind her. Once inside, she took Lana's coat and hung it in the closet, then motioned for her to follow her into the kitchen. She poured them both a glass of merlot and decided maybe sitting at the kitchen table was a better idea than retiring to the living room.

"This is a nice house," Lana said once they were settled.

"It's okay," Court said with a slight shrug. "Not much privacy, though."

"Nosy neighbors?"

"Nosy younger sister who lives next door." Court grinned at the thought of Lori and her two young children. "Either she or her kids are over here a lot when I'm home."

"I hope you're close, or else it could get rather awkward."

"We are. I was five when she was born, and we lost our mother a year after that." Court looked away when she saw sorrow in Lana's eyes. "I was always Lori's protector when we were growing up."

"I'm sorry about your mother," Lana said.

"She committed suicide," Court said without much emotion. It had been hard to deal with when she was finally old enough to know the truth about her mother's death, but it was far enough in her past now to not be painful. "She suffered from post-partum depression after Lori was born, and she never recovered from it."

"Did your father ever remarry?"

"No, he raised us on his own. He did a pretty good job of it too, if I'm being honest."

"Does he live nearby?" Lana asked before taking a sip of her wine.

"He died five years ago. Cancer." His death was still new enough to cause Court to think she'd start crying whenever she talked about him, so she swallowed around the lump in her throat. "He didn't get to see me win the gold medal in the last Olympics."

"I'm sure he would have been very proud of you."

"He was proud of me," she answered with a nod and a fond smile. "I thought he was going to burst when we won the bronze four years earlier. That was before he found out he had cancer."

Court desperately wanted to change the subject, because she hated feeling on the verge of crying. Especially in front of someone she hardly knew.

"So," Lana said after a moment. "No girlfriend, right?"

"No," Court said, grateful for the change in subject. "Not in quite some time, actually."

"I find that hard to believe."

"The longest relationship I've ever had was three months."

"Why? Is there really something wrong with you?" Lana smiled, no doubt to soften her words, and Court laughed.

"I don't think so," she said with a shrug. "It always came down to me being too driven to play hockey. Nobody likes to play second fiddle to a game, and I can't say I blame any of them."

"That's absurd," Lana said. She set her glass on the table and sat back in her chair. "Are you saying they didn't know what they were getting into when they started dating you?"

"I doubt it, since I usually met them at the arena after a game." Court sighed and leaned back in her own chair. "I guess they all just thought since the women's game doesn't pay enough to actually make a living, I'd give it up for them."

"Why are you so driven to play?"

"My dad. I know it probably sounds crazy to you, but I feel closer to him when I play." Of course the conversation would lead back to him. Why wouldn't it? Court smiled as she recalled memories about him. "He always pushed me to be the best I could be, and he taught me everything I know about the game. He always rearranged his schedule to be able and see every game I played, even the ones on the road. So even now, when I step out on the ice, I like to imagine he's there in the stands, cheering me on. I can't give that up as long as I'm still able to play."

"It doesn't sound crazy," Lana said, shaking her head. "I think it sounds amazing. And I think you're amazing. Any woman would be lucky to be with you."

Court felt her cheeks flush and she looked away as she scratched the back of her neck. She glanced at the clock on the wall and saw it was almost eleven. She needed to get to bed soon.

"It's late," Lana said as though she could read her mind. She stood and took her glass to the sink to rinse it out. "Could you give me a ride to the pizzeria?"

Court nodded and led the way to the front door. The attraction she felt to Lana was incredibly strong, and she had to fight her instincts telling her Lana felt it too. If she gave in and kissed her, she had a feeling she wouldn't be getting any sleep. And with a morning skate scheduled before they got on the bus to head to Philly, she definitely needed the sleep.

❖

"I honestly didn't expect to see you back here tonight," Joey said when Lana walked through the doors.

"I told you it was just a meeting," Lana said. He was closing up, and she grabbed a broom to help clean the dining area.

"With a hot woman," he said with a laugh.

"Stop."

"Mom called a little while ago. Why didn't you tell her you were looking for another place to stay while you're here?"

"I wasn't going to until I found a place and signed the

paperwork, which I did tonight. I figured I'd let her know in the morning."

"Now you don't have to. She already knows."

"Wonderful." Lana stopped sweeping and turned to look at him. "Why did she call? Is Eric all right?"

"He's fine." Joey waved her off before taking the cash out of the register. "She wants us to go with her to the hospital in the morning. Dad's getting restless, and she wants a united front to try to convince him he needs to stay put and follow doctor's orders."

"Since when has he listened to anything any of us tell him? He's as stubborn as a mule." Lana finished sweeping and followed him into the kitchen area to clean up there while he got the bank deposit ready. "You take after him in that department, you know."

"Me?" Joey said, sounding incredulous. "Mom says you're the one who inherited his stubborn streak."

Lana thought about it for a minute and decided her mother was probably right. One of the reasons she'd agreed to come home while her father was recuperating was to try to repair her fractured relationship with her parents. They weren't getting any younger, and this heart attack drove home the fact. She thought back to Court telling her about losing both her parents, and she felt her eyes welling up. What she wouldn't do to have her father be proud of her.

She wasn't foolish enough to think it would ever happen, though.

CHAPTER NINE

When Lana got back from dropping Eric off at school the next morning, she barely had enough time to drink a cup of coffee before their mother was ushering them out the door to go to the hospital. Lana had been back in town for almost a week, and she'd only been to see him once. She felt bad about it, but she just didn't know how to talk to her father. Of course, on the other hand, he didn't know how to talk to her either. It was almost as though they were both afraid of pissing the other one off.

As a result, Lana sat in a chair a few feet from his bed while Joey and their mother tried to reason with him while standing at his bedside. Reasoning with him had never been an easy thing to do.

"You need to talk to the doctor and tell him I want to go home," he said emphatically even though his voice sounded weak.

"Pop, you need to get better, all right?" Joey said calmly. "You know if you went home you'd want to have a hand in everything that's going on. You'll never get better if you don't rest, and this is the best place for you to recover."

"Lana, come here," her father said. She was so taken aback to hear him say her name, she didn't react right away. Joey and their mother stepped away and looked at her. He reached his hand out to her. "Come here, *tesoro*."

The term of endearment caught her off guard. He hadn't used it since before she'd come out to them. She stood slowly and went to his side, taking his hand in hers. She was surprised his grip was so strong as he held on tightly. She glanced at Joey, who looked as shocked as she felt.

"Tell them I'd do better recovering at home," he said with a pleading look in his eyes.

"I can't, Dad," she said quietly. He dropped her hand and turned his head away before waving her off. She looked at her mother, who gave her a quick nod and a tilt of her head in his direction. Lana cleared her throat and grasped his hand again. If she wanted to repair their relationship, she figured there was no better time to start than now. "Dad, listen to me. You and I have had our differences over the years."

"Understatement," Joey said, not quite under his breath, but Lana chose to ignore him.

"We've gone too long without speaking," she continued. "You're my father, and I love you. You need to get better, because you have a grandson who wants to get to know you. If the doctors think you should stay here in order to heal, then you've got to do it. I'm helping Joey with the pizzeria, and Eric's been helping Mom around the house. You don't need to worry about anything but getting better, all right?"

She waited a few moments, but he refused to look at her or even acknowledge anything she'd said. She let out a sigh and released his hand before picking up her jacket and telling Joey she'd be in the cafeteria.

He could be so infuriating sometimes. She wondered

briefly even why she'd want to repair a relationship with him. But damn it, he was family. Eric didn't really know them, and they were the only family he had. She was sitting at a table in the cafeteria staring into her coffee when she felt a hand on her shoulder.

"Are you all right?" Gail Crawford asked, a look of concern on her face. "If you want to be alone, I'll understand."

"I'm sorry. Please have a seat," Lana said with a forced smile. "What are you doing here?"

"I just came by to see one of my players before we left for Philly," Gail said as she settled into her seat.

"Jen Hilton?" Lana asked.

"Yeah, she has a concussion, and the doctor's releasing her today, but she won't be able to play for at least a couple more weeks." Gail took a sip of her own coffee and looked at her. "I just wanted to see how she was doing."

"Not sure I could force myself to be nice to her considering what she did in that game before she got bowled over."

Gail nodded, and Lana sat back in her chair.

"Yeah, I can't deny the entire team is pretty pissed at her for what she did. I am too, but for better or worse, she's a part of the team, and we all need to figure out how to make it work."

Lana wondered how difficult it would be to accomplish. It was obvious Jen Hilton didn't like Court, and she was pretty sure the feeling was mutual.

"When are you leaving for Philly?" Lana waited as Gail looked at her watch.

"In about an hour," Gail said as she got to her feet. "Which means I need to get going or I'll miss the bus. I hope your father is well enough to go home soon."

"Thank you." Lana forced a smile and watched as Gail walked out of the cafeteria. She let out a sigh and placed her elbows on the table, her head resting in her hands. She couldn't wait to move into her new house. At least she'd be moved before her father made it home.

"He's going to stay," Joey said as he sat in the chair across from her. "I think what you said to him hit home."

"I doubt it," she said with a snort.

"I know you think he doesn't like you, but you're wrong."

"They both said they accepted it when I came out, but I know they don't approve of my lifestyle, and they'll never understand it. I'm sure both of them would have been perfectly fine if I hadn't come home to help out."

"Then why did you?"

"Because you asked me to, Joey," she said quietly. He had to know that, didn't he? She knew their parents would never have told him about the arguments they'd had before she'd left for college, but she also knew he wasn't stupid. He was the same age then as Eric was now, and he had to have sensed the tension between her and their parents.

"Is it the only reason?" he asked.

She looked away and shook her head.

"I know they won't be around forever," she said after a moment. "And like I said to him earlier, I love them, and I do want Eric to know his grandparents. I guess I hoped there was a chance we could heal this rift between us."

"They love you, too, you know," he said as he reached across the table and took her hand. She started to tell him he was wrong, but he didn't let her. "They do. They always ask me how you're doing, and Dad even made me sit at the computer with him one night so we could research you on the internet. It was almost like he couldn't get enough information. We also read a few articles on Eric. He's a pretty decent hockey player from what I understand."

"He is," Lana said with a fond smile. She hadn't really wanted him to play when he first approached her about it, but she decided to indulge him. He'd been eight at the time, and they'd just watched the women win the bronze medal in the Olympics, so his interest was at a fever pitch. She made a compromise with him—if he still wanted to play when he was ten, she'd let him. Of course he did still want to play, but she figured one season and he'd be done. Little had she known he'd fall in love with the game. Or that he'd be so damn good at it. "He probably won't be going to college. He's got junior teams scouting him, and he could be drafted next year."

"Wow," Joey said, smiling like the proud uncle she assumed he was. "Is it the Canadian Hockey League?"

"No, there's a junior league in our region," she said, wondering not for the first time if it wouldn't be better for them to be living here permanently so he could have a shot at a major junior team in one of the three leagues in the CHL. It would be an amazing opportunity for him, she knew that. But if she'd moved them here and he did get taken in the Quebec Major Junior Hockey League draft, he would have to move to Quebec and live with another family anyway while he finished high school and honed his skills for a possible career in the NHL.

"Is he going to play while he's here?"

"We've been looking for a team. They don't play in too many high schools here, so it's been a little bit of a challenge, but yeah, he definitely wants to play."

"We should probably get back to his room," Joey said after they'd talked about Eric and hockey a little more. "Mom will start to think we left without her."

She nodded and got up to follow him, trying not to think too hard about what he'd told her about their father researching her on the internet. If it was true, then maybe there was a chance for them to find some kind of common ground.

CHAPTER TEN

The pizzeria wasn't busy at all the next night, and it gave Lana and Eric the opportunity to sit in the kitchen and listen to the Warriors game on the radio.

"I can't believe she has two goals already," Eric said at the end of the first period. It was good to see him so excited about something. Lana had been worried he would be sullen and withdrawn the entire time they were here. Who could have guessed Court Abbott would be the reason they'd both feel good about having to live in Kingsville for a few months? "I hope she gets a hat trick."

"That would be great," Lana said in agreement.

"Aren't you two here to work?" Joey asked.

"Go round up some customers and we will," Lana said with a smirk.

"Don't rub it in," Joey said as he pulled up a stool and joined them. The bell at the front door would alert them if they had a customer, so there was no need to worry about pissing anyone off. "So, are you dating her?"

Lana almost laughed at how fast Eric's head swung around at the question. Ever since he'd been old enough to ask questions about why she and his father weren't together, she hadn't tried to keep her sexuality a secret from him. What would be the point? They had a great relationship, and he felt comfortable talking about anything with her. She never offered information about her personal life, but if he asked, she didn't lie to him about anything.

"You and Courtney Abbott?" he asked, a decidedly hopeful tone to his voice. "Seriously?"

"No, we aren't dating," she replied, her heart aching a little at the disappointment she saw in Eric's expression. He wanted her to find someone and to be happy. He hadn't been shy about voicing his opinions on the matter since the day he'd turned thirteen.

"Bummer, because that would be so awesome."

"So awesome," Joey agreed, and they gave each other a high five as Lana shook her head at the two of them.

She happened to agree with them, but she wasn't about to admit it out loud. She went to grab a slice of pepperoni before the second period started and smacked Joey in the back of the head as she walked past him.

"Why so interested in my personal life?" she asked.

"Well, I'm considering making a commercial for the pizzeria, and I was thinking it would be good for business to have a local celebrity be our spokesperson," he said, rubbing his head where she'd hit him. "You'd be surprised how many young kids look up to her."

"And you thought I could help you talk her into it?"

"Well, yeah." His tone made it clear he thought it was obvious.

"You could just ask her on your own, you know." Lana resumed her seat just as the puck was dropped.

Joey started to say something else, but Eric held his hand up, his eyes glued to the radio. Court had won the faceoff and the Warriors were on the attack. He let out a whoop she'd never heard from him before and he pumped his fist in the air. She'd only seen him use that particular fist pump for his favorite player on the Blackhawks, Patrick Kane.

"Hat trick!" he said with a single clap, and then he rubbed his hands together. "How great is she?"

"She's pretty great," Joey said with a wink for Lana behind Eric's back. She shook her head. It was apparent he wasn't buying it when she said they weren't dating. He probably thought she didn't want to admit it in front of Eric. Lana vowed to set him straight on her relationship with her son.

The game ended with a 5–2 score, and Eric didn't stop talking about Court the entire time they were going through the closing routine for the pizzeria. Joey wasn't any different, though. If she didn't know better, she'd have thought her little brother had a crush on Courtney Abbott.

"When are we moving into the house?" Eric asked on the ride back to her parents' house.

Lana had hoped to be moved in over the weekend, but Eric had a tryout with a local team earlier that day, and tomorrow she'd promised her mother she'd help her clean the house. They'd only been there for a couple of weeks, but she couldn't wait to move into their own place.

"Tomorrow night, I think," she answered. It wasn't like they had a ton of stuff with them, but the car had been pretty packed on their drive from Chicago. She was hoping to get it done in one trip, but it was probably more realistic to do it in two. At least it was only a fifteen-minute ride. "Can you handle one more night with Grandma?"

"She's not so bad," Eric said with a shrug. "Except she's always trying to kiss my cheek and hug me. It's a little creepy."

"I can imagine." Lana tried to stifle a laugh but wasn't successful. Eric laughed with her.

"She's not happy we're leaving."

"We aren't *leaving* exactly," she said, feeling exasperated. "We're just moving into our own space a few minutes away."

"That's what I told her." Eric yawned. Lana looked at the clock and fought back a yawn of her own. It was almost eleven. He was quiet for a few minutes, and she was starting to think he'd fallen asleep. He startled her when he spoke again. "Maybe we should invite Court over for dinner in our new house."

"Maybe," she answered thoughtfully. It wasn't like she hadn't thought of the idea herself, but she was surprised Eric suggested it. "You like her, huh?"

"What's not to like?" he asked.

Indeed, she thought with a small smile.

"You think she might help me with my passing game?" he asked.

"I'm sure it wouldn't hurt to ask her." Lana glanced at him in the passenger seat next to her.

He was a gifted player, and had been told so by any number of people who knew better than she did. The one thing he always had a problem with, though, was passing the puck. He was sloppy most of the time, and he'd worked harder on that aspect of his game than any other in the past couple of years.

The coach for the team he'd tried out for that day told him if he could make crisper passes to his line mates, he'd be unstoppable. He'd said a player who scores, but can't set up his teammates for their own goals, probably wouldn't make it very far. He needed to be more than a one-dimensional player if he truly wanted to make it to the next level.

Lana knew he took every bit of advice to heart, and he had improved some, but he wasn't quite there yet. He'd made the team today, and he was ecstatic about it, but he knew he needed to do something to get even better still. She had no doubt he could do anything he put his mind to. If he wanted to improve, he would. She hoped for his sake Court would be willing to give him some pointers.

"Maybe you should invite her over Monday night," Eric said.

"I don't know." Lana wasn't sure how to respond. Of course, she wanted to do exactly that, but what if Court turned her down? What did it really matter anyway? It wasn't as though she and Eric would be around past the end of the school year. Not that either of them would be interested in something long-term, but it just seemed wrong somehow to try to start something with Court. She shook her head at the way her thoughts were going in so many different directions. "I don't even know when they'll be back from their road trip."

"Tuesday, then," he suggested.

"I'll think about it, okay?"

It was the best she could do at the moment. She didn't want to get his hopes up, because it was becoming apparent he was enamored with Court, even if it was just the possibility in his mind that she might date her.

CHAPTER ELEVEN

It had been a good road trip. Actually, it had been a great road trip. They'd won both games, and Court had scored a total of seven points. There'd even been a crowd of people waiting at the arena to welcome them home when the bus pulled in that afternoon.

"Somebody here to see you, Abbott," Savannah said as she took a seat in front of her locker.

"An angry one-night stand?" Kelly asked in a teasing tone.

"Not unless she's started dating teenage boys," Savannah deadpanned.

"Who is it?" Court asked, ignoring their banter.

"Some kid who no doubt fell in love with you because of all the points you got over the weekend," Savannah answered with a shrug. "He didn't give me his name."

They didn't have a practice scheduled, but most of the team tried to get at least a skating session in every day. She finished lacing her skates and pulled on her practice jersey and helmet before standing and closing her locker. She grabbed her stick and headed for the door.

"He's behind the bench," Savannah called out. "You can't miss him. Cute kid."

Court ignored the laughter she heard from them as she exited the locker room. As she headed down the hallway to the ice, her mind frantically tried to think who it might be. The last person she thought of was Lana's kid.

"Shit," she muttered, looking down at her feet as she stepped onto the ice. "What the hell is his name? Eric?"

She headed for the bench and stopped short of the boards. He was smiling at her, but he also looked a little nervous to be standing there.

"I hope it's okay for me to be here," he said after a moment.

"Where's your mom?" she asked, taking the time to scan the area and seeing no one else but him. She met his eyes. "You're Eric, right?"

The joy lighting up his face because of the simple fact she remembered his name caused a reaction she hadn't expected in herself. She couldn't help but smile back at him as she felt her heart warm.

"Yeah, but she isn't here."

"Does she know you're here?" Court asked. "Shouldn't you be at school today?"

"We get out at two thirty," he answered. "And yes, she knows I'm here."

"What can I do for you?"

He looked up at the glass surrounding the playing surface and the bench area, then seemed to be looking around the arena for a break in it somewhere. There was none, and Court sighed. Her teammates would be out soon, and she really didn't want to be having a loud conversation with him when they did. She motioned for him to walk down to the end of the rink and the doors where the Zamboni came out to clear the ice between periods.

"Hey!" she called out to a maintenance guy who was eating his lunch. She waved him over when he looked up at her. "Open this for him, please?"

She took Eric's arm so he wouldn't slip and fall on the smooth ice surface and led him over to the bench. They sat side by side and Court removed her helmet after leaning her stick against the boards in front of them.

"What can I do for you?" she asked again.

"I made a team," he said with a grin. "And they're letting me have number eight."

"That's great." She was happy for him, but she doubted he was here just to tell her about making a team.

"I was wondering if you could help me with something," he said, looking down at his feet.

"Is talking to you always like pulling teeth?" She realized she sounded harsh and wished she could take the comment back. To her surprise, he chuckled and glanced at her.

"My mom used to say that about me."

"I was just kidding," she said, nudging him with her elbow and wondering whether or not he believed her.

"I was hoping maybe you could help me become a better passer." Her hesitation must have worried him, because he started talking again right away. "I pretty much suck at it, honestly. I have a good shot at being picked pretty high in the junior draft next spring, and if I could improve my passing game it would really help a lot."

"I could probably help you," she said as her teammates started coming onto the ice. "Your mom has my phone number. Give me a call tomorrow and we can work out some details."

"Awesome!" he said with a huge grin. "Thank you so much."

He got up to leave and realized he was kind of stuck there on the bench.

"Come on," she said, leading him back onto the ice.

"Hey, I almost forgot," he said as they got to the gate where he could leave. "My mom wanted me to invite you for dinner."

"Tonight?" Court asked, unable to hide her surprise. It was a nice surprise, but a surprise nonetheless.

"If you're free?" he asked, his tone hopeful. "Or tomorrow, maybe?"

"I'm free tonight," she said before she had time to think too much about it. "What time?"

"We usually eat at seven."

"I'll be there."

"Okay then, I'll see you later," he said, walking backward and smiling at her.

"Yeah," she said. "Later."

She shook her head and skated to the other end of the ice where Savannah and Kelly were waiting for her.

"Did he ask you on a date?" Savannah asked, and they both doubled over in laughter.

Court laughed at their good-natured ribbing, and she responded with the truth.

"Yes, actually, he did," she said, thoroughly enjoying the looks of shock on their faces. "And before you ask, I accepted. Dinner tonight. At his house."

She skated backward, laughing at their expressions.

"With him and his mother." She howled at them when they looked at each other, obviously not believing her, but she didn't care. Was it a date, with Lana of course, or was it just dinner with a friend? Lana would have asked herself if it was a date, right? She decided to shove it from her mind and concentrate on what she was doing. She'd find out tonight.

❖

"Who is this woman, and why have you never mentioned her before?" Court's sister, Lori, said as they sat on her couch. She'd gone to Lori's to get advice, but realized upon reflection it was a bit ridiculous to ask for dating advice from a woman who had two kids by two different men and had never been married.

"She's here to help her family. Her father had a heart attack."

"So she's from here?"

"Originally, yeah," Court said, glancing at the clock. She only had about fifteen minutes to talk if she wanted to make it to Lana's on time. "She's leaving at the end of the school year to go back to Chicago."

"Well, then, there's your answer," Lori said, slapping her on the thigh. "A fling seems appropriate given the circumstances."

"You're a big help." Court sighed.

"Okay, how about this," Lori said, undeterred by Court's irritation as usual. "She probably isn't someone you should even think about getting involved with if she uses her son to invite you to dinner. Whether it's a fling or…maybe something more?"

"It can't be more," Court said again, feeling as though she were speaking to her seven-year-old nephew. "I *just* told you, she's leaving at the end of the school year. Not to mention I have a contract with the Warriors for another season after this one."

"It's October," Lori said. She looked at Court like she thought she was dense. "School doesn't end until late May or early June. A lot can happen between now and then, Court. I really don't think you need me to tell you that."

"I should go." Court stood and walked toward the door. "Tell the kids I love them, and I'll see them tomorrow."

"Court," Lori said as she stood and hurried over to her. She hugged Court and kissed her on the cheek. "Just let whatever happens happen, okay?"

"Yeah, okay." Court smiled and headed outside to her car. Maybe Lori was right. She was probably thinking too hard about things, and she should just let it happen. Or not happen, whatever the case may be.

Chapter Twelve

Court stood on the porch wondering what the hell she was doing. Twice on the drive to Lana's she'd almost turned around and gone home. And now she was considering it once more. She tightened her grip on the bottle of wine she held in her hand and glanced back at her car.

"What the hell am I doing?" she muttered as she took a step toward the door. She shook her head and laughed at herself. Being nervous about having dinner with a beautiful woman had never happened before. Then again, she'd never been invited to dinner by the beautiful woman's son before either.

She'd agreed to help Eric with his game, so even if this turned out to not be a date with Lana, she could use the time to talk to him about hockey. Set up a plan to work together. There was no reason to be nervous. Before she could overthink things anymore, she raised her hand and knocked on the door before her.

That was when the panic really set in. She heard noise coming from the other side of the door, and she contemplated her odds of being able to get to her car and speed away before anyone saw her. Her breath caught in her throat when the door opened, and she found herself standing face-to-face with Lana, who seemed genuinely surprised to find Court on her porch.

"Courtney Court?" she asked, her head tilted to the side and a small smile tugging at the corners of her mouth. "What are you doing here?"

"Um…" Court was confused. Perhaps she'd misunderstood Eric. "Eric said you wanted him to invite me to dinner."

"He did?" Lana looked to be confused too, but she stepped aside for Court to enter. "I'll have to have a talk with him later."

"I'm sorry. Should I not be here?"

"No, it's fine," Lana said, shutting the door. She hung Court's jacket up and then motioned for her to follow her into the kitchen. "When did you talk to Eric, if you don't mind me asking?"

"He came to the arena this afternoon. He said you knew he was coming to see me." Court shook her head as she handed the bottle of wine to Lana. Lana's reaction to all this made her realize she'd been duped. "You didn't know, though, did you?"

"No, I didn't."

"I'm sorry," Court said, feeling like an idiot for falling for it. "I should go."

"Court, no, please stay. You don't have anything to be sorry for." Lana gripped her wrist when Court turned to leave. "I know he wanted to talk to you about possibly helping him with his passing game, and we talked about inviting you for dinner sometime, but I didn't know he was going to do any of it today. I would never use him to ask you out. If I were going to ask you out, I would do it myself."

"Good to know." Court relaxed a little and made a mental note to remember it in the future.

"Would you like some?" Lana asked as she held up the bottle of wine.

"Yes, please," Court said.

"Unfortunately, I only have plastic cups." Lana laughed. "I haven't had time to do much shopping for anything."

"I don't mind." Court leaned against the counter and watched as Lana opened the bottle and began to pour it. "I see you have a corkscrew, though."

"A corkscrew is essential for life," Lana said, giving her a look indicating anyone should know that. "I am never very far from my trusty corkscrew."

"Thank you." Court accepted the plastic cup Lana offered.

"I should be thanking you." Lana touched her cup to Court's and smiled. "To unexpected, but very welcome, dinner guests."

"I really feel like kind of an idiot," Court said after taking a sip. "I should have called to make sure it was okay."

"There's something you need to know about Eric." Lana took a lasagna out of the oven. She turned to face Court and smiled, which caused Court's stomach to flutter. "If hockey doesn't work out for him, I think he has a second calling as a matchmaker."

"So he's done this before, I take it?" Court felt a stab of jealousy, and shook her head with a chuckle to hide it. It was so not like her to be jealous. Especially when she wasn't even involved with the woman in question.

"Oh, yes. More than once, and not just with me." Lana took Court by the arm and led her to the living room, where they sat next to each other on the couch. "He's done it with a few of his friends as well. His matches have never worked out for me, but he's been fairly successful with people his own age."

"I guess that means you and I won't work out, then?" Court said the words in jest, but she realized as she spoke she really wanted it to work out. There was something about Lana pulling her in. Something she didn't want to fight. The look Lana gave her made her breath catch.

"Oh, Courtney Court." Lana took Court's cup and set it on the end table next to hers before turning to face her. She took Court's hands in her own as she spoke. "You know I won't be in town forever. I'm not sure it would be wise for us to get involved."

"Did you forget the part where I told you I've never had a relationship last for more than three months?" Court gave Lana her best self-deprecating smile.

"Maybe we should eat," Lana said, but she didn't release Court's hands.

Court wondered what the hell she was doing. She'd never had to try to talk a woman into becoming romantically involved. In fact, she'd never even had to pursue a woman at all. They always came to her. So why did she feel more intent than ever on convincing Lana?

❖

Lana filled their plates with food and sat across from Court at the kitchen table. She couldn't believe Eric had put her in this position and then made sure he wasn't around when Court arrived. She couldn't deny she was attracted to Court, but she wasn't entirely certain getting involved with her was wise. She had a feeling it would be difficult to remember she'd need to keep her heart protected.

They both looked up when they heard the front door open, and Lana set her fork down on her plate. Court looked uncomfortable when their eyes met, and Lana placed a hand over hers and squeezed gently.

"Eric?" she called as she released Court and sat up straighter. "Could you come in here, please?"

"Hey, Mom," he said with a grin. At least he had the decency to be embarrassed when he saw Court sitting there with her. "Hi, Court."

"Hi."

"I think you owe Court an apology," Lana said, one eyebrow raised to let him know she was serious. "And to me also. We've talked about this before."

"I'm sorry," he said, but he was looking down at his feet instead of at Court.

"Not good enough," Lana said. "Apologize to Court."

"It's okay," Court whispered to her, but Lana shook her head once to let her know it wasn't.

"I'm sorry, Court," Eric said, raising his head to look directly at her. "I shouldn't have told you my mom wanted me to ask you over for dinner tonight."

"Thank you," Lana said before picking up her fork again. "Have you eaten?"

"I had a slice of pizza at Caruso's after practice."

"Then go to your room. We'll talk about this later."

"Mom," he said, his voice on the edge of whining.

She simply looked at him, daring him to defy her. She'd never been able to stay mad at him, and he knew it, but she also knew he wouldn't want her to embarrass him any further in front of Court. He sighed and nodded before turning and leaving the kitchen.

"I'm sorry he lied to you," Lana said.

"It's really okay," Court told her as she began eating. "I'm having dinner with a beautiful woman, so I'd say it's worked out pretty well."

"Well, aren't you the charmer?" Lana tried to ignore the fluttering feeling in her chest. Unfortunately, it was next to impossible to not notice it was affecting her more than she wanted it to. "I'm still going to have a chat with him about it, though."

"We have a game Wednesday night," Court said after a few moments. "Will you come? And let me take you for a quick bite to eat after?"

"Courtney Court, are you asking me out on a date?" Lana stared at her, not quite believing what she was hearing from this incredible woman who just a few days earlier was having trouble even flirting with her.

"How do I answer to get you to say yes?"

"I think you just answered perfectly."

Court smiled and nodded, causing a feeling of euphoria to wash over her. She was entering uncharted territory with Court, but she wasn't sure she could stop it even if she'd wanted to.

❖

"Thank you for dinner," Court said as she put her jacket on to leave around nine o'clock.

They'd sat on the couch talking for a while after they were finished with dinner, and then Lana had called Eric to join them so he and Court could hammer out some details for his training sessions with her. Lana wasn't ready for the evening to end, but she was thrilled she'd be seeing Court again on Wednesday.

"You're welcome," she said, feeling nervous. Was Court going to try to kiss her? Should she try to kiss Court? She'd never wondered about things like that before. She'd also never wanted to kiss someone so badly. "We should do it again sometime."

"I'd like that," Court said.

Lana stepped toward her, and she was a little disappointed when Court leaned in and kissed her on the cheek. Court smiled and turned to walk out the door, leaving Lana wanting for more. But she'd seen the way Court looked at her, and knew she wasn't alone in her desire. That was something, right?

She headed back to the living room where Eric was waiting for her, no doubt knowing he was going to get a talking to. She sat next to him on the couch and took his hand.

"I know your heart is in the right place, honey, but you have to stop trying to set me up with dates. I can get my own dates."

"I know, Mom, but I really like her, and I wanted her to help me with my game."

"She said she would, right? She doesn't need to be dating me in order to do it."

"So, you don't like her?"

"I do like her," Lana admitted. She laughed at how quickly his look of disappointment turned to excitement. "But it doesn't make what you did okay, you know that, right?"

"Yeah."

"What if I didn't like her, but she liked me?" Lana asked him. "You'd have put me in a very uncomfortable position. You can't play with people's emotions like that."

"I know, and I'm sorry," he said, sounding sincere. "I promise I won't do it again."

She studied him for a moment and finally nodded, coming to the conclusion he really meant what he was saying. She patted his knee and sighed.

"I hope you won't."

She also hoped she could manage to keep her heart from being broken. She just needed to keep reminding herself she was leaving, and not let Court too close. She could do this.

Chapter Thirteen

C ourt skated to the bench before the game started and looked up to see Lana watching her. She smiled and Lana waved. When Court returned her gaze to the bench, she saw Gail watching her, a smirk on her face.

"What?" Court asked, sounding defensive even to her own ears.

"Nothing," Gail replied, shaking her head.

Court chose to ignore her for the time being, because she knew Gail would corner her later and want all the details about what was going on between her and Lana. Court and her line mates, Savannah and Kelly, stood at the blue line for the national anthem. When it was over, she couldn't resist another glance at Lana, who seemed to be watching her intently.

"You want to go out after the game?" Kelly asked as they skated around center ice waiting for the puck drop to start the game. "Savannah and I are going to Allentown."

"I have plans," she answered with a shake of her head.

"Not with a teenage boy, I hope," Savannah said, causing them all to laugh.

"No, with his mother."

Court hadn't expected it, but her words managed to shut

them up. Court grinned as she put the blade of her stick on the ice and began jockeying with the opposing team's center in anticipation of the puck drop.

Court could tell the game was going to get out of hand when the officials made it clear they were going to just let them play and only call the most blatant of penalties. When she got cross-checked hard enough to knock her to her knees and they still didn't call it, she started to lose her temper. Someone was going to get hurt if they kept calling the game this way.

They made it through the first period without any major incidents and a two-goal lead, but Gail pulled her aside once they were in the locker room.

"This is bullshit, Gail," she said, barely resisting the urge to throw her helmet across the room.

"I know," Gail said, her exasperation obvious. "Complaints from both benches are falling on deaf ears, though. They seem determined to let the game go on like this."

"What do we do?"

"I don't want us to start anything, but I don't want to back down from anything either," Gail said, both of them looking at the room full of women trying not to let their frustrations get the better of them. Gail met Court's eyes and nodded once. "Hopefully, the other team will use the same approach, but if not, you ladies know how to handle yourselves."

Court hated fighting. It wasn't allowed in most of the women's leagues, but this one was trying to develop into a league that played more like the men, and as a result, there were more people in the stands, which meant more money in everyone's pockets. She loved a good hard hit in the corner as much as the other players, but fighting took away from the game, in her opinion. However, when frustrations ran as high as they were tonight, a good old-fashioned skirmish was inevitable. She nodded her understanding and headed toward her locker.

"What the hell's going on out there tonight?" Savannah asked.

"They're letting us play hockey," Court answered as she ran a hand through her hair before turning and facing the rest of her team. "Listen up, ladies. If the officials aren't going to call a clean game, we need to take matters into our own hands. Don't go looking for a fight, but if one comes looking for you, deal with it however you feel is best."

Usually, as a team, they avoided melees, which tended to piss the other teams off because they almost always ended up taking penalties, and the Warriors had the best power-play unit in the league. They all understood it was inescapable at times, though. It looked like tonight was probably going to be one of those times.

"We *have* to fight?" asked someone from the back of the room. Court didn't recognize the voice, but she shook her head at all of them.

"Nobody's telling you to fight, but nobody's saying you have to turn the other cheek either. Nobody on this team will *ever* tell you you *have* to fight."

"Let's go win this game," Kelly said, standing and putting her helmet back on. She clapped Court on the back. "And I'll do everything I can to keep that handsome face of yours from getting pummeled, seeing as you have plans for tonight."

"Thanks," Court said with a chuckle. "I appreciate it."

Midway through the second period, Court had a breakaway. She skated fast, managing to stay a couple of strides ahead of the closest opposing team member. Just as she was about to let a shot go, she was slashed in the shins and went down, slamming hard into the boards. She stayed down for a few moments, taking stock of everything. Nothing really hurt other than her shins, which wasn't surprising since they'd shattered the stick of the player who slashed her.

She heard a lot of yelling to her left where Savannah and Kelly were involved in a shoving match with a couple of players from the other team. Court waved off the trainer who was starting to make his way out to her and got to her feet to an eruption of cheers from the fans. She was pushed from behind as she started to skate away from it all and everything seemed to fade away except for her frustration and anger.

She turned and saw a woman sneering at her, standing a couple of feet away. She watched as the woman dropped her gloves and removed her helmet. Court did the same without even thinking about what was happening. The other woman threw the first punch, which caught Court right below her left eye. Fuck, that hurt, but she wasn't about to show any weakness. Court landed the next two, and the woman ended up flat on her back holding her nose between both hands.

"You fucking bitch!" she yelled, but made no move to even try to get up and come after her again.

Court glanced around and saw a couple of other fights in progress, and officials trying to break it all up. She didn't feel the least bit sorry for them, though. They were the ones who'd allowed things to get to this point.

She skated toward the bench and touched the spot under her eye that stung like hell. She pulled her hand away and her fingers were covered in blood. Gail handed her a towel when she got to the bench and she pressed it to the spot. Once the fights had all ended, she skated to the locker room with the trainer so he could stitch her up.

"How are you doing?" Gail asked when the team came in after the period was over.

"It's gonna leave a mark, that's for sure," Court said.

"You broke her nose, so there's that, right?" Gail said with a slight grin. She squeezed Court's shoulder briefly. "You might as well get dressed. We're up by four, and I can't risk you getting seriously injured."

"Eight stitches," the trainer said while he finished cleaning up the mess. "You should be good to go, Court."

"Thanks, Lou," she said before he walked away.

"Get dressed and go spend the rest of the game with your girlfriend." Gail's singsongy teasing tone made Court shake her head.

"Not my girlfriend."

"Sure she isn't, Abbott," Kelly said as she walked by. "You should have seen how worried she looked when you left the ice."

"Seriously, Court," Gail said when Kelly was out of earshot. "What's going on with you and Lana Caruso?"

"Nothing." Court stood from the table she was sitting on, bracing herself in case she felt a little woozy. She let out a sigh of relief when she didn't. "We enjoy spending time with each other."

"She has a kid," Gail said, teasing her again.

"It's not like I'm looking to marry her or anything," Court said, feeling a little on edge. "We haven't even kissed."

"Yet."

Court watched Gail turn to walk away, and she couldn't help but chuckle to herself.

"Yet," she said under her breath. But she was definitely hoping it would happen sooner rather than later.

❖

"Oh, my God, Court, are you okay?" Lana asked, her voice full of concern, when Court took a seat next to her in the stands. "It looks like it hurts."

"I'd be lying if I said it didn't," Court answered with a shrug. "But I'm fine."

"Then why are you up here and not out there playing?"

"Because the game is pretty much over, and Gail doesn't want me hurt any more than I already am."

"You'd better not be lying to me." Lana caught her gaze and held it, silently daring Court to argue with her. She gently touched Court's cheekbone with her fingertips but pulled away quickly when Court closed her eyes for a moment. "I'm sorry if I hurt you."

"You didn't," Court assured her with a wink, which apparently did hurt if her wince was any indication.

"Should we get out of here?" Lana asked. She had the indescribable desire to take care of Court, not to mention the fact she was afraid she might not be able to keep from kissing her if they were to sit there much longer.

"I have to stay until it's over," Court told her with a glance at the scoreboard. The Warriors were up five to nothing with ten minutes left to play. "It's in the standard contract. Unless you're in the hospital, you have to be here for the games."

"Okay." Lana couldn't say she was happy about it, but she smiled slightly when Court reached over and took her hand. At least she wouldn't have to wait around for her to shower and get dressed after the final buzzer went off.

CHAPTER FOURTEEN

Lana had never been on a date with a woman who held her hand as they walked and opened doors for her. She decided she kind of liked it. She smiled at Court when she held the car door open for her. They'd decided to take one car from the arena and Court would take her back to get her car after they got something to eat.

"You're probably sick of pizza, aren't you?" Court asked as she pulled out into traffic.

"I love pizza," Lana answered, a little surprised at the question.

"I thought maybe since your family owns the pizzeria you might have been forced to eat it a lot growing up."

"I'll admit we did have it more than anyone else I knew, but it could be why I still love it so much now." Lana put her head against the back of the seat and looked at Court as she drove. She sighed. Court was beautiful, and she took the time to really study her while she was busy keeping her eyes on the road. Her hair curled up slightly in the back. Just about halfway down her neck. She turned slightly in her seat and reached over to touch the curls. She knew she shouldn't have done it, but she couldn't help herself. She smiled when Court glanced over at her. "Does this bother you?"

"No," Court said, returning her eyes to the road in front of her. "Well, yes, but not the way you're thinking."

Lana laughed out loud and moved her hand to Court's thigh. As she moved it slowly toward Court's center, running her fingernails along the seam of her jeans, she stifled a moan when Court shifted slightly in her seat. Court's hand covered hers quickly and moved it back toward her knee.

"I'm sorry," Lana said, putting her hands in her own lap, sitting up straighter, and looking out the windshield. "I'll try to behave myself."

"Only because I don't want to get in an accident," Court said quickly, glancing at her again. "God, if I wasn't driving…"

"I'll keep that in mind," Lana said, turning her hand over when Court reached for it. She watched as their fingers intertwined, and wondered silently to herself what exactly she was doing.

Court was a distraction. A very attractive, charming, and desirable one, but still, it was dangerous to think of her as any more than a disruption to her incredibly boring life while living at home for a few months. As long as Court understood how things were, there shouldn't be a problem, right?

"Lana?"

She blinked, and noticed Court had parked a couple of blocks down the street from Caruso's. She looked around and shook her head to get rid of the cobwebs.

"I'm sorry, what did you say?"

"Where were you?" Court was smiling at her, and Lana returned it.

"Just thinking. Nothing important."

"It didn't look that way," Court said, sounding like she

didn't believe her. And why should she? Lana was lying, after all.

"I promise," she said with a squeeze of Court's hand. "Please don't tell me you're taking me to Caruso's on our date."

"No," Court chuckled as she unbuckled her seat belt. She pointed at a bar just up the road a few feet. "This place has the best burgers in town. I assumed burgers would be a safe choice since you made the lasagna with ground beef. Which was excellent, by the way."

"Thank you, and burgers are perfect." Lana smiled when Court jumped out of the car and was at her door before she could even think about undoing her own seat belt. Lana took the hand she offered to help her out of the car, and when she tried to release her, Court held on. She looked at her, one eyebrow raised in question.

"I like touching you," Court said softly. "Is that a problem?"

"No," Lana answered, even though she thought it could very well turn into a problem. She resolved to not think about it tonight though. Tonight, she just wanted to see where things took them and worry about what it might mean some other time.

❖

"You were right. Those burgers were amazing," Lana said when they were back in the car.

Court headed back to the arena so Lana could get her car, but it wasn't really what she wanted to do. She wanted to take Lana home and spend the night with her. They'd sat close together throughout their meal and touched each other, on the hand, the leg, the arm, a lot. Court was trying to ignore the pulsing between her legs, but it was rather insistent. She shifted slightly to relieve the pressure that was rapidly becoming uncomfortable.

"Thank you for having dinner with me tonight," she said.

"Thank you for inviting me," Lana answered with a sigh. "I enjoy spending time with you."

"Me too." Court thought about asking her what she wanted to do now, but decided taking her back to her car was the best course of action. *Keep it light, and see where it goes.* She pulled into traffic and headed back toward the arena.

"Can we walk for a bit?" Lana asked when they pulled in behind her car.

"Yeah, sure," Court said with a nod. She got out and went to open Lana's door for her, but Lana beat her to it. She took Lana's hand when she held it out to her. They walked in silence for a few minutes, looking in the windows of the shops that were closed for the night all along the main street of Kingsville.

"This town always reminded me of Bedford Falls," Lana said.

"From *It's a Wonderful Life?*" Court asked. They stopped in front of a coffee shop and Court studied Lana's reflection in the glass.

"Yeah." Lana turned and smiled. "All the little shops and businesses. There's a lot of small town charm here, you know? Where did you grow up?"

"Allentown. Not a lot of charm there, small town or otherwise."

The wind gusted, and a lock of hair obscured Lana's eyes. Court brushed it away from her face and Lana smiled at her. Court let her hand linger against Lana's cheek and moved her thumb across her bottom lip. Because she wasn't sure what Lana wanted, she let her arm drop and looked down the street.

"Hey," Lana said, grabbing Court's shirt in both fists and pulling her closer. "You can't do that and not kiss me."

"Really?" Court grinned at her. "Did I miss that in the instruction booklet?"

"You must have."

Lana stood there, Court's shirt in her grasp, and just stared at her. When her tongue darted out to moisten her lips, Court thought for sure her knees were going to give out. She put her hands on Lana's hips and pulled her closer.

"You're sure I have to kiss you?" she asked.

"It's a rule." Lana nodded. "If you don't, then there can't ever be a second date."

"Oh, well, when you put it that way…"

Court touched her lips to Lana's, lightly at first, just to test the waters. When Lana's hands released her shirt and moved up her neck to hold her in place, Court moaned. She skimmed Lana's lips with her tongue, and Lana parted her lips to allow her entry. As soon as her tongue slid along Lana's, she felt light-headed. She broke the kiss and took a step back.

"Why did you stop?"

Court looked around and noticed a small alleyway next to the coffee shop, so she grabbed Lana by the hand and led her there quickly. She turned, fully intending to press Lana against the wall, but Lana was quicker. Court, her back against the building, smiled as Lana moved in, taking her mouth in a searing kiss that threatened to send Court over the edge right there. Her body tingled with the anticipation of what Lana could do to her if they didn't have clothes in the way. She was in danger of finding out if she didn't put some distance between them. She turned her head away to break the kiss, and Lana's lips began working on her neck.

"Stop," she said weakly. She didn't really want Lana to stop. She was just afraid someone would find them. Probably a cop, and she really didn't want to end up in jail. Lana pulled away and looked in her eyes. "God, I want you."

"Then why stop?"

"Um, because we're outside? In the middle of town?" Court said, laughing. "I think we need to go somewhere else to continue this. Will you come home with me?"

Lana took a step away from her and shook her head. "I can't. I have to pick Eric up at the pizzeria."

Court's disappointment must have been obvious because Lana smiled and pressed her fingers to Court's lips.

"It isn't that I don't want to continue this, because I think it's pretty apparent I do," Lana said. There was just enough light from the street for Court to see Lana's eyes as they roamed shamelessly over her body. Lana shook her head and closed her eyes. "Jesus, I can't believe I'm saying no to you right now. Next time?"

"When?" Court asked, sounding just a little too desperate. Honestly, she didn't care. "Where?"

"Tomorrow night?" Lana said. "Your place?"

"Yes," Court said. "Tomorrow is perfect."

"Time?"

"Does six work for you?"

"I'll be there at six. Should I bring anything?"

"All I need is you."

"Good answer," Lana said before giving her a quick kiss on the lips and then turning and walking away, leaving Court alone in the alley to compose herself.

Court let her head rest against the building behind her and she stared up at the sky. She wondered if a fling with Lana would ever be enough. She supposed unless she wanted her heart broken, it would have to be.

CHAPTER FIFTEEN

Court looked at the clock on the stove again and wiped her sweaty palms on the legs of her jeans. Lana would be there any minute. She checked the table one more time, making sure she'd put everything out. She'd never been much of a cook, but she could make hot dogs and hamburgers with the best of them. She figured that type of fare would be a little too juvenile for what she was hoping would be a romantic dinner, so she'd picked up some Chinese takeout on her way home from a property showing.

Her pulse spiked when the doorbell rang, and she stood there, frozen. This was ridiculous. There was nothing to be nervous about. She ran her hands through her hair and took a deep breath before forcing herself to walk to the front door. When she opened it, she just stared at Lana standing there looking more beautiful than any woman Court had ever laid eyes on.

"Hi," Lana said with a shy smile. She looked down at herself and then back to Court. "I wasn't sure how to dress. I hope this is okay."

"More than okay," Court managed. Lana was wearing a

pair of tight-fitting jeans and a turquoise sweater snug enough to leave no doubt of the fact she was a woman. Court's brain finally engaged and she held out her hand and urged her inside. "I'm hoping you won't be dressed for long anyway."

She tried to pull Lana closer, but Lana took her hands and threaded their fingers together "We have all night, Courtney Court. There's no need to rush things."

"Right." Court nodded and looked down at their hands as she tried willing her pulse to return to a normal rate. "I got dinner."

"Good. Dinner's good."

They sat and ate as they talked about mundane things. Court was feeling strangely like she did as a teenager on her first date with another girl. It seemed she had only one thing on her mind, and it didn't appear Lana was on the same page. She was beginning to think maybe it had been for the best when Lana put the brakes on the previous night, but then Lana stood and held her hand out. Court took it and allowed herself to be pulled to a standing position.

"Can we sit and talk for a little bit?" Lana asked, looking a little nervous for the first time since she'd arrived.

Funny, but seeing Lana nervous helped Court to relax. Court led her to the living room.

She watched her as Lana's eyes landed on the framed Olympic medals and Team USA jerseys on the wall above the couch.

"Wow," Lana said, walking toward them. She reached out and touched the frame, then smiled as she glanced at her over her shoulder. "This is impressive."

"I guess so," Court said, feeling her cheeks heat in embarrassment. She'd always been uncomfortable talking about her achievements. Her father had taught her to be humble. To not brag about the things she accomplished, because bragging was an unattractive trait to have. "I'll admit it was a lot of fun playing on a world stage."

"Why aren't you playing in the Olympics this time around?" Lana took a seat on the couch and removed her shoes. She patted the cushion next to her, and Court sat as well.

"I was invited to camp, but I came to the conclusion I'd done what I could for Team USA," Court said. It hadn't been an easy decision to make, but Gail had spent many evenings hashing it all out with her, and they'd both agreed. "There are a lot of women who would love to make the team, and for me to keep hanging on would just take a spot away from someone else. Someone younger. I know I wouldn't have been happy as a twenty-year-old if I lost a spot to someone who was in their mid-thirties and not nearly as fast or as talented as she used to be."

"I don't know if I could be so gracious," Lana said. "Especially when it seems to me you haven't diminished in the skills department. There's been what? Ten games so far this season? You have twelve goals and sixteen assists."

"You've been keeping track?" Court met her eyes and gave her a smirk.

"No," she answered hesitantly. "Eric is a bit of a stats nerd, and I think he has a bit of a crush on you."

"That could be awkward, but not very believable," Court said. "Remember, he tried to set us up on a date. It doesn't sound like something someone with a crush would do."

"Okay, fine." Lana let out a sigh. "I think you might be his new hero."

Court didn't know what to say in response. She stared at Lana for a moment. Despite her long-held reservations about getting involved with a woman who had children, she had to admit Eric was making her seriously rethink things. He seemed like a really good kid.

"We'll see if he still feels the same way after I try to help him with his game," she finally said.

"I don't think it's going to change anytime soon." Lana leaned back and crossed her legs. Court reached out and placed her palm on Lana's thigh, because, well, she *had* to touch her. "I think you might be stuck with him."

"So do you know my plus-minus number?" Court asked when Lana covered her hand with her own and moved it a few inches up on her thigh. "Average ice time per game? Penalty minutes? Faceoff percentage?"

"No, so I hope you don't tell me talking hockey stats is an aphrodisiac for you," Lana said. "But if it is, I can certainly study up on your statistics for our next date."

Lana turned her head to look at Court and tentatively touched her cheek, right below the stitches she'd received the night before. Court closed her eyes and leaned slightly into the touch.

"Your eye is a beautiful shade of black," she said, trying not to laugh but failing.

"Better than a broken nose," Court said with a chuckle.

"You broke her nose?"

"I did."

"Good. She deserved it."

"You probably haven't dated many women with black eyes, have you?"

Lana placed a hand firmly on her shoulder and pushed her down on her back. She heard Court's quick intake of breath when she began to unbutton her shirt.

"That would be a pretty safe assumption," she said, meeting Court's gaze. God, what was it about her? Lana wasn't usually the aggressive type, but after she'd slowed things down when she arrived earlier, she'd gotten the distinct feeling Court was waiting for her to make the first move. Once the shirt was unbuttoned, she smoothed her palm across Court's taut abdomen, eliciting a moan, which only ratcheted up her desire. "You are so fucking sexy, Court."

She'd never dated a woman who was an athlete, and she was impressed by the chiseled muscles that appeared to be barely contained beneath Court's skin. Her body was hard, but strangely soft at the same time. The dichotomy was fascinating to her. She met Court's eyes as she pushed her sports bra up to free her breasts. Her breathing quickened at the feel of them in her hands and she finally broke their eye contact so she could lean down and take a nipple into her mouth.

"Lana," Court said, her breath as uneven as Lana's was. "Lana, look at me." Lana stopped what she was doing and did as Court asked. "As much as I don't want to stop this, I really think we should move this party upstairs. The bed is much more comfortable than this crappy piece of furniture I bought at a yard sale."

She nodded and got to her feet, but she clasped Court's hand and didn't let go as she followed her up the stairs. She was afraid if she let go, the spell between them would be broken. It was ridiculous, she knew, because it was obvious what Court wanted. Once in the bedroom, Court got on the bed and urged Lana to stretch out next to her, facing each other.

She closed her eyes when Court ran her hand through her hair and urged her closer for a kiss. Even though her body wanted fast and urgent, she tried to force herself to remain in control of her faculties when Court's tongue ran slowly across her bottom lip.

Any semblance of control went out the window when Court reached down and grabbed the back of her leg and pulled it over her body so Lana was straddling her. Their kiss never broke, though, and their tongues were involved in a slow battle of control when Lana ran her hand up Court's side and cupped her breast, her thumb lightly grazing the nipple just below the edge of the sports bra she hadn't yet removed.

"Oh, my God," Court murmured when she pulled away so they could both catch their breath. "I think this might be the most fun I've ever had with my clothes on."

Lana straightened her body and leaned back against Court's bent legs. Court's hands went to her hips and encouraged her to move them slowly across her abdomen. Once she started, she knew she wouldn't be able to stop. Court moved her hands under her shirt and gently squeezed Lana's nipples through her bra, causing what felt like a jolt of electricity straight to her already swollen clit. She pressed her hands against Court's to hold them in place and met her eyes as her hips continued to move faster.

"Don't you dare stop what you're doing," she said breathlessly.

"Come for me, Lana." Court's breaths were coming in short bursts much like her own. "Please."

Lana fell forward, her hands on either side of Court's shoulders, and she forced herself to move her hips more slowly, enjoying the delicious feeling of the seam in her jeans pressing against her sex. Her forehead pressed against Court's shoulder when it felt like she was about to explode from the inside out.

"I'm about to come," she said into Court's ear. Court's arms went around her waist and held her tightly as Lana went over the edge. Nothing else existed in that moment other than the two of them, and the feel of Court's solid body pressing against hers. She was aware she was moaning her pleasure as her hips jerked in an attempt to milk every last bit of her orgasm. When her body finally went slack, she felt Court's lips against her temple. After a moment, she rolled off Court and onto her back, an arm across her eyes. "I'd have to agree with your earlier assessment. This is definitely the most fun I've ever had with my clothes on. Or even with my clothes off, if I'm being honest."

Court chuckled and propped herself up on an elbow to look down at her. She removed the arm Lana had over her eyes and then let her hand move down her neck to her chest.

"Agreed, but I think we need to try it naked," Court said. "I really think I need to taste you."

"Jesus," Lana said, squeezing her legs together against the onslaught of feeling those words evoked. And the look in Court's eye. Like she wanted to devour her. *Fuck.*

She watched as Court got to her feet and quickly stripped all her clothes off as Lana did the same with her own shirt and bra. Lana crossed her arms behind her head and tried not to come undone when Court unbuttoned her jeans and pulled them, along with her underwear, slowly down her legs and finally dropped them to the floor. Once they were both naked, Court's hands started at Lana's feet and moved up her legs as she crawled onto the bed. Lana closed her eyes and allowed her legs to fall open for Court.

She was still sensitive from her first orgasm, and she bucked when Court spread her lips with her tongue.

"Too soon?" she asked, looking up at her.

Lana met her eyes and was struck by the eroticism of the view she had. She didn't trust herself to speak, so she reached down and put her hand on the back of Court's head, urging her to finish what she started.

Her second orgasm came so quickly she wasn't prepared for it. She cried out as her head pressed back into the pillow, and her hips lifted off the bed. Court slid her fingers inside her and never stopped what she was doing and succeeded in drawing a mind-blowing third orgasm from her body.

"Come here," Lana said, her voice raspy. She felt tremors run through her body as Court slowly withdrew her fingers and crawled up to lie down next to her. She turned and put an arm across Court's torso, holding her tightly as she waited for her breathing to return to normal. "That was amazing. You're amazing, Courtney Court."

Court chuckled as she shifted so her arm was around Lana's shoulders and Lana's head was nestled against her neck. Lana pressed her lips to Court's collarbone and sighed contentedly.

"Twenty-six," Court said after a few moments.

"What?" Lana said, having no clue what she was talking about.

"My plus-minus statistic," Court said.

"Smart-ass." Lana pinched her side and Court laughed.

"Coincidentally, it's also my average ice time per game."

"Good to know," Lana said, feeling her limbs grow heavy.

"Good night, Lana."

"I just need to rest for a minute," she responded, having every intention of reciprocating. "There are some things I have to do to you too."

The last sound she heard was the deep rumble of a laugh coming from Court's chest not far from her ear.

CHAPTER SIXTEEN

Court woke up the next morning in the same position she'd been in when she'd fallen asleep. Lana was still in her arms, an arm slung across her torso, and a leg hooked around one of hers. She took in a deep breath and then tried to lie still when she felt Lana stir.

"Oh, my God," Lana said, her voice husky from sleep. She rolled onto her back and stared at the ceiling. "I feel like such a guy for falling asleep on you. Literally."

"I'll take it as a compliment seeing as how I obviously satisfied you enough to make you sleep so soundly," Court said with a cocky grin.

"I bet you say that to all the girls," Lana said as she peeked at her from under her arm and smiled.

No doubt the smile was meant to assure Court she was teasing her, but the comment only served to make her uncomfortable. She couldn't recall ever uttering those words before. In fact, there was rarely a morning after with the women she slept with. Her MO was to leave before anyone fell asleep. She wasn't sure why, but it suddenly seemed important for Lana to know the truth. She turned over to face her and laid her palm on Lana's stomach.

"You'd lose that bet," she said softly. When Lana moved her arm and looked at her, Court shook her head. "I've never said it. To anyone. Ever."

Lana didn't immediately say anything in response, but her eyes softened, and she placed a hand on Court's cheek. She smoothed her thumb over the cheekbone below her stitches.

"Are you for real?" she finally asked.

In lieu of an answer, Court moved her hand up to cup her breast as she leaned over and kissed her. She'd meant it to be a simple peck on the lips, but Lana apparently had other ideas. Her hand went to the inside of Court's thigh and moved slowly toward her center.

"What time is it?" Lana asked when she broke their kiss.

Court glanced at the clock and felt a moment of panic until she remembered she didn't have to be anywhere until after noon. She shifted so her legs opened to give Lana the access to where she needed her to be.

"Eight o'clock," she said, her pulse spiking as she felt Lana's fingers lightly brush her clit before moving downward and sliding easily inside her. "Oh, yes."

"Do you have to be somewhere?"

"No," Court answered, her eyes sliding closed as she allowed herself to feel nothing but Lana's fingers pumping her slowly. It felt so good.

"Good," Lana said before placing a quick kiss on her lips and then she took an erect nipple in her mouth.

"Shit," Court muttered when Lana's thumb pressed against her clit at the same time her tongue flicked her nipple. She spread her legs wider when Lana's thumb started pressing her clit each time she thrust her fingers into her. Her tongue ran along Court's skin until she reached her ear.

"Tell me what you want, baby," she said.

"I want this," she managed to say. "You on top of me. I want to come with you inside."

"Now tell me what you *need,* Court."

"You. Everywhere. Please." Court placed a hand on her ass and urged her to lay on top of her as her hips began to move in unison with Lana's thrusts. She lifted her head to capture Lana's lips, her tongue sliding sensually along Lana's before sucking on her bottom lip. "Oh, God, you're gonna make me come."

Lana didn't change her pace at all, and Court buried her face in Lana's neck as she felt herself tightening around her fingers. One last thrust and she cried out her pleasure, her hips bucking wildly, but Lana managed to keep up with her movements.

"Jesus Christ," she said when the feeling finally subsided. She looked up at Lana. "That was...wow."

"Wow, huh? Is that the best you can do?"

"When my mind is blown? Yeah." Court was pleased her response got a laugh out of Lana, but she was disappointed when Lana rolled off of her and got out of the bed. "You have to be somewhere?"

"Not until eleven," she responded on her way to the bathroom. "I have to help Joey with the lunch rush today."

"Are you a coffee drinker?" Court asked. She sat up but didn't immediately get to her feet. She wasn't entirely sure her legs would support her quite yet.

"A cup of coffee would be amazing," Lana said before closing the door behind her.

Court finally stood and grabbed her clothes from the night before to throw on quickly. On her way down the stairs she heard a knock on the front door. When she opened it and saw Lori standing there, she glanced back toward the staircase.

"Morning, sis," Lori said, walking in without an

invitation. Court supposed she should be happy Lori knocked. Usually she just let herself in, which wasn't a problem normally. She never had overnight company before. "I hope you have coffee, because I ran out. Whose car is in your driveway?"

"I was just about to make some coffee," Court said, following her into the kitchen. She started to get it ready, but then stopped and turned to face her. "You can't stay, because I have company."

"Company?" Lori seemed shocked, which didn't surprise Court. "Since when do you bring a woman home with you?"

"It's Lana, okay?" Court blew out a breath in exasperation.

"Lana?" Lori asked, looking like she didn't know who Court was referring to. "Oh, the one from the pizza place? The one who's moving back to Chicago with her *child* in a few months?"

Court turned back to get the coffee ready, not wanting Lori to see her irritation. Like she needed anyone to remind her she didn't date women with kids. She pushed the button and willed the coffee to finish brewing before Lana made her way downstairs. Unfortunately, that didn't happen.

"Good morning," she heard Lori say, sounding overly cheery.

"Good morning," Lana replied, sounding wary. Court turned to face them both and leaned against the counter, her arms folded over her chest.

"You must be Lana," Lori said.

"Apparently, I'm out of the loop." Lana looked at Court and then back to Lori. "You know who I am, but I don't know who you are."

"Are you going to introduce us?" Lori asked Court.

"Lana Caruso, this is Lori Abbott, my little sister," Court said.

"Oh," Lana said, feeling relief flood through her. For a moment she worried it might be a girlfriend. Which was stupid, because jealousy wasn't something she should be even remotely experiencing, was it? "You live next door, right?"

"I do," Lori said, turning her attention to Court then. She batted her eyes and Lana somehow kept from laughing. "You talked about me?"

"Only about how annoying it is when you show up at inopportune times."

"You're both dressed," Lori pointed out. "I'm willing to bet there were more inopportune times earlier."

Lana watched with amusement as Court poured a cup of coffee and put it on the counter in front of her sister. Court annoyed was kind of cute.

"Here's your coffee," Court said. "You can go now."

"Are you always this grouchy first thing in the morning?" Lori shook her head when she took her cup and walked over to Lana. "It was nice meeting you."

"You too," Lana replied. When she was gone, Lana looked at Court again, who she caught staring at her.

"I'm sorry about that. She really needs to learn how to call ahead before she comes over."

"It's okay," Lana told her. Court filled another cup and gave it to her. "She was right, though. There were certainly more embarrassing times she could have shown up."

Lana knew they should talk about things, but thought it might be too soon. Reminding Court how this couldn't go beyond the next few months would probably diminish what they'd shared, and she really didn't want to do that.

"What does the rest of your week look like?" Court asked.

"I've been helping Joey during lunch, and Eric's been working for him at night." Lana took a seat at the breakfast bar and put some sugar in her coffee. "What are you doing tonight?"

"Babysitting," Court said, rolling her eyes. "Lori has a date tonight."

"How old are her kids?"

"Five and seven." Court looked at her and smiled. "We'll be having hot dogs with macaroni and cheese if you want to stop by. Oh, and we'll probably be watching *Frozen*. Again. For like the thousandth time."

"For Eric it was *Toy Story*." Lana laughed and shook her head. "I think there was a time I could have recited the entire movie in my sleep."

"I know the feeling."

Lana watched her as Court scratched the back of her neck and stared into her coffee for a few moments. She looked as though she were unsure of herself, and it made Lana want to wrap her arms around her. She never thought Court would be unsure or nervous about much of anything.

"What time is dinner?" she asked before taking a sip of her coffee.

"Six. Movie at seven, and they're usually asleep before the movie's over."

Lana nodded. Eric had to work at six, so she could drop him off on the way over and pick him up on her way back home. It would probably be more exciting than spending the evening at home alone. She stood and took her cup to the sink, stopping on the way to place a hand on Court's forearm.

"No promises, but I'll see what I can work out." She kissed Court on the cheek before slapping her ass playfully. Court put an arm around her waist and pulled her close. Lana did her best not to fall into the blue eyes she was staring into. "Be careful there, Courtney Court. I just might want to take you back to bed, and I really don't have the time this morning to do everything to you I have in mind."

"I'll see you tonight," Court said after giving her a quick kiss on the lips and releasing her. She let out a sigh. "Maybe?"

"Maybe."

CHAPTER SEVENTEEN

The lunch rush was dying down when Joey pulled Lana into his office. He'd been looking at her strangely since she'd arrived promptly at eleven, but hadn't said anything to her. Lana knew she'd been smiling all morning, but she couldn't help it. Court was amazing.

"What's going on with you today?" Joey asked her after closing the door behind them.

"I don't know what you're talking about."

"Really? You've had a goofy-looking smile plastered on your mug ever since you got here."

"No, actually it's been there for much longer."

It was almost comical when it dawned on him. His eyes went wide, and his jaw went slack. He sat back in his chair and pointed at her as he nodded.

"You got laid." Lana didn't say anything, but just sat there watching him. "You said you wanted Eric and me to bond last night, but you really just wanted him out of the way, didn't you?"

"I wouldn't put it that way exactly," Lana said.

"It was Court Abbott, am I right?"

"Maybe."

"Did you ask her about being in my commercial?"

"Sorry, but the subject never came up."

"When are you seeing her again?"

"Tonight. Maybe."

"Will you promise me you'll talk to her about it?"

"I'm not going to promise anything." Lana got up and walked to the door. She stopped and turned to look at him before going back out to the kitchen. "You're a big boy, Joey. I'm sure you can figure out how to ask her yourself."

She finished her shift and headed home until it was time to pick Eric up from hockey practice. She was in the process of cleaning the house when her phone buzzed in her pocket. She pulled it out and smiled when she saw it was a text from Court.

How many hotdogs can u eat?

She wondered briefly if she should reply with something flirty, but decided against it.

Pretty sure of yourself, aren't you?:)

She chuckled to herself when she hit the Send button and sat down to wait for the response. It only took a few seconds.

No, just optimistic

I like optimism. I can eat 2 hotdogs

Cool. I'll see U later then?

Yes

Lana leaned her head back against the couch and sighed. Why couldn't she have met Court in Chicago? It had been strange, yet surprisingly wonderful, waking up in her arms that morning. Strange because it was so out of character for her to spend the night with anyone, at least since Eric had been born.

She blew out a breath and shook her head. Wanting things that weren't going to happen was pointless. But fantasizing was harmless enough, wasn't it?

❖

"Hey, Mom," Eric said after stowing his gear in the trunk. He slid into the passenger seat and buckled his seat belt before leaning over and kissing her on the cheek. She smiled at him but didn't say anything. She remembered a time when he hadn't wanted anyone to see him kiss his mother. She was happy he seemed to have finally outgrown that phase. He looked at her through narrowed eyes. "What?"

"Nothing," she said with a shake of her head before pulling away from the curb outside the ice rink where his team held their practices and games. After a moment, she reached over and ran her fingers through his hair. It was still wet from the shower he'd taken after practice. "I thought it was really uncool to be seen giving your mother a kiss."

His cheeks turned slightly red and he turned to look out the window. He shrugged as he spoke. "It is, if it's on the lips. A peck on the cheek is okay."

"I see."

"Am I spending the night at Grandma's again?"

She tried to gauge his feelings on the matter, but he was still facing away from her and she couldn't see his face.

"I'm not planning on it," she told him. "Why? Do you want to?"

"Not really." He looked at her then. "I mean, I don't mind, but I'd rather not. I am old enough to take care of myself for a few hours in the evening, you know."

She glanced at him, knowing he was a young man now, but not quite sure how to reconcile the thought with her image of him as her little boy. They talked about everything, because her parents had talked to her about *nothing*. She wanted her relationship with Eric to be absolutely nothing like the one she had with them. As a result, he'd always known he could ask her anything, tell her anything, and she would always do her best to answer his questions. And he also knew she'd be there for him, no matter what.

"I do know that, Eric," she said quietly.

"Wait, it wasn't just a few hours in the evening, was it?" He was staring at her. She knew he thought if he stared long enough she'd squirm under his scrutiny, but she refused to react. Apparently, he didn't intend to let her non-response discourage him. "Did you stay out all night?"

Lana did squirm a little then. She wasn't sure how to answer him, but she'd never lied to him before, so there was no point in starting now. She took a deep breath and looked at him again. She was met by a big smile.

"Were you with Court?" he asked.

"Eric, I—"

"Mom, come on," he said in mock exasperation. "You told me all about the birds and the bees almost three years ago."

"Only because you asked," she pointed out. "It wasn't my choice to tell you anything about sex at only thirteen years old."

"Not relevant," he said. "I know all about sex."

"You'd better not." She was thankful she'd arrived at Caruso's. She pulled into the parking lot and cut the engine. "Are you having sex?"

"No, I'm not, and don't try to change the subject."

"Yes, I was with Court." She felt her cheeks burning and looked away from him for a moment. "But your grandmother would have a stroke if she knew we talked about these things, so you can never say anything to her about knowing *all about sex*, understand?"

"Yeah," he said, ducking his head. "But just so you know,

I like her. I'll be happy to stay the night at Grandma's anytime you want to spend time with Court."

He kissed her cheek again and gave her a goofy smile. She had no idea how to respond to his statement, so she just kept quiet. He looked as though he were going to say something else, but then shook his head and got out of the car. Before closing the door, he leaned down and looked at her.

"Are you seeing her again tonight?"

"For dinner and a movie," Lana said with a nod. "I'll be here to pick you up at ten."

"Or I could just go home with Uncle Joey again," he said. "Just throwing it out there."

"I'll be here at ten."

He shrugged and closed the door. She watched him as he crossed in front of the car and waved at her. He probably didn't believe her, but her mother really would freak out if she knew she talked about these things with her son. She sighed and started the car again. She could just make it to Court's by six if she hurried.

CHAPTER EIGHTEEN

Court looked at the clock on the stove for what felt like the fiftieth time. Why the hell was she nervous? So Lana was coming over for dinner and babysitting. What was there to be nervous about? She wiped her palms on the legs of her jeans and jumped a little when the doorbell rang. She laughed at herself as she realized this was a déjà vu moment from the night before.

"Can I answer, Aunt Court?" Ryan, her seven-year-old nephew, asked. She heard him running from the living room toward the front door as he was talking.

"Wait for me," she said. Three steps got her to the door the same time he arrived. She stood to the side and motioned for him to open it. "Go ahead."

"Who's there?" he asked, looking up at her. She gave him a thumbs-up. She and Lori had been working on teaching him not to just open the door to anyone.

"Um, Lana?" came the voice from the other side. Court smiled at the uneasy tone.

Ryan looked at her, and she nodded. He used both hands to turn the knob and stood back as the door swung open.

"Hi," he said with a wave before running back to the living

room where his sister was still sitting on the floor playing with her dolls. Court chuckled as Lana walked into the house.

"He just likes to open the door," she said with a shrug. "He hasn't learned yet what to do after that."

"He's cute," Lana said, allowing Court to help her out of her coat.

"Now he is," Court agreed. "Wait until I tell him it's bedtime. I swear he turns into the devil when he has to do something he doesn't want to do."

Court led the way into the kitchen where the hot dogs were just about done. She turned to look at Lana but almost ran right into her. Lana's hands went to her waist, and Court grinned. "Sorry."

"Don't be," Lana replied. Court leaned in to kiss her, and Lana pressed her body tighter against her.

"Hi," Court said, pulling away slightly. She brushed a lock of hair off Lana's forehead. "How was your day?"

"Other than my brother giving me the third degree about where I was last night?" Lana pulled away from Court and leaned against the counter. "It was okay. How was yours?"

"Great." Court grabbed some mustard, ketchup, and relish from the fridge and then started putting out hot dog buns as she talked. "I woke up feeling better than I have in a long time, and spent a little time with an incredibly beautiful and sexy woman before I had to go to work. I sold a house, so there's that too. But it all pales in comparison to the morning, if I'm being honest."

"Stop." Lana blushed when Court turned her head to look at her.

"What?"

"You can't talk to me like that with young children in the house." Lana gave her a small smile. "I can't be responsible for what happens if you do."

Court put down the food she was holding and went to Lana. She stood close to her, her hands on the counter on either side of Lana's body. They were both breathing a little heavier than normal, and Court kissed her quickly on the lips.

"And you can't tell me that when you know there's nothing I can do about it." She grinned and looked toward the door. "Or I could just make them go to bed now."

"You're bad," Lana said, but she was smiling as she slapped her lightly on the shoulder.

"You have no idea." Court closed her eyes against the onslaught of arousal as she rested her forehead against Lana's.

"God, the things I want to do to you," Lana whispered.

Court heard both kids stomping through the living room, so she pulled away reluctantly before they caught them in a compromising position. It wouldn't matter really. They knew Court liked women instead of men, because Lori didn't see any reason to hide it from them.

"Hold that thought," she said before turning back to the food.

"Aunt Court!" Ryan said. "We're hungry!"

"Let's get you in your seats and I'll bring the food to you." Court leaned down and picked up her five-year-old niece, Alice. She stopped in front of Lana and looked down at Alice. "Can you say hi to Lana?"

Alice turned her head and buried her face in Court's neck. Court rubbed her back gently and gave Lana an apologetic smile.

"This is Alice. She's a little shy, as you can see."

"Hi, Alice," Lana said, but Alice refused to look at her. She met Court's eyes. "It's okay."

Lana was surprised at how well behaved the kids were while they were eating their hot dogs. When Eric had been their ages, he seemed to be more interested in throwing his food than eating it. Which wasn't to say they didn't make a mess. Alice had more food on her clothes than she'd probably managed to get in her mouth, and Ryan had mustard and ketchup all over his face.

Court got the movie ready to go while Lana cleaned Ryan's face, then Court took them to get their pajamas on before they settled in to watch. Lana took the time to look around the living room since the night before her perusal had been halted after seeing the Olympic medals and then by activities on the couch she probably shouldn't be thinking about, if the surge of arousal was any indication. There were a lot of pictures on the wall of a younger Court with her father, most of them with Court in her hockey uniform. It was obvious by his smile in all of them that he was proud of his daughter.

She ran a hand along the well-used blanket thrown over the back of the couch and took in the furnishings. The couch looked comfortable even though she knew differently from the previous evening, but the recliner next to it was obviously Court's favorite place to sit as she relaxed and watched television. It was leather, but the seat was well worn. She sat in it and leaned back with her eyes closed, her hands running along the arms of the chair.

"You're in Aunt Court's spot," Ryan said, causing her to open her eyes and lean forward. Lana saw Court standing behind him, Alice in her arms. Ryan pointed at her and looked at Court. "She's in your spot!"

"She's okay, buddy," Court told him as she got them situated on the couch.

"But you don't let me sit there." Ryan scowled at her and crossed his arms.

"I told you I'd let you sit there when you're older, didn't

I?" Court was kneeling in front of him and her hands were on his knees as she spoke. He nodded, but it didn't look to Lana as though he was happy about having to agree with her.

"She's new," he said quietly. "I'm not."

Lana decided she should probably get up and hopefully make it easier for Court to defuse the situation. She walked past and met Court's eyes as she disappeared into the kitchen. She hadn't considered she might not be welcomed by the kids. As far as they were concerned, she was an interloper. They probably loved the time they got to spend with Court, and she was taking it away from them. She'd decided to just go home when Court joined her in the kitchen.

"I should go," Lana said.

"What? No." Court shook her head and closed the distance between them, her hands resting on Lana's hips. "He's okay now. The movie's playing, and it will all be forgotten before Elsa even creates Olaf."

"Are you sure?"

"He's just not used to having to share me," Court said, sounding reluctant to admit it. "He's never seen me with anyone before."

"Never?" Lana knew she sounded skeptical, but she didn't believe it could be true. Court had never brought a girlfriend around? Ever? The realization should have made her uneasy, but instead, it simply caused a fluttering sensation in her chest. She couldn't think straight with Court looking at her as though she intended to rip her clothes off and take her right there against the kitchen counter.

"Never," Court said before kissing her lightly on the lips. Her hands went under Lana's shirt and moved up her sides. Lana bit back a moan when Court's eyes darkened. "Do you think they'd notice if we disappeared upstairs?"

"Don't tempt me." Lana laughed and pushed her away, even

though all she wanted was Court's hands on her. Everywhere. And her lips. Jesus, her lips were amazing. She shook her head to try to gain some semblance of control. "You're bad."

"But you like it, right?" Court grinned, and Lana thought it was the sexiest thing she'd ever seen. She took Lana by the hand and pulled her toward the living room. "Come watch a movie with me."

Lana started out sitting next to Court on the couch, but Alice wormed her way between them before curling up and falling asleep in Lana's lap. Lana missed this—having a small child in her arms. Not that she wanted another one. Eric was all she needed, and she was too old to be thinking about raising another one.

Both kids were asleep before the movie was over, just as Court had predicted. Court picked Ryan up, and Lana followed with Alice, to take them into the spare bedroom upstairs. Once they were tucked in, they went back to the living room. Lana looked at the clock and saw it was just before nine.

"Want to make out?" Court asked. Lana laughed at the way she waggled her eyebrows.

"I'm not sure it would be wise," Lana answered as they resumed their seats on the couch.

"Come on. I'll make it worth your while."

"I have no doubt." Lana took her hand and held it in her lap, her thumb moving back and forth across her skin.

"Hey, are you okay?" Court put an arm around her shoulders and urged Lana to lean against her very solid body.

"I'm better than okay," Lana said. But was she? It wasn't wise to be feeling things for Court. They really needed to talk about what was going on between them. It wasn't a conversation she was looking forward to.

"Will you stay the night with me again?"

Lana sighed and pulled away from her. She needed her

distance in order to say what she needed to say. She met Court's eyes and shook her head.

"I can't. I have to pick Eric up at work in about an hour. I can't make him stay with my mother again." Although he did say it would be okay...*no, this is not going to become a habit.* "I have to be a responsible parent."

"Maybe this weekend, then?"

"We should talk," Lana said, and the change in Court's demeanor was instant. She sat up straighter and looked away from her. Lana took her hand again and didn't let her pull it away. "Listen to me, Court. I like you. A lot. And I think you know I want to be with you again."

When Court looked at her, Lana nodded and smiled. She touched Court's cheek with the back of her hand, then ran her fingers through her hair.

"But?" Court asked, sounding like she didn't really want to hear whatever else Lana had to say.

"But I'm not going to be here—in Kingsville—forever."

"I know."

"I need to know you're okay with it, though." Lana had the fleeting thought that she was speaking more to herself than she was to Court. She'd be wise to heed her own words.

"I am," Court said, moving closer to her again. "I know you'll be gone before summer. You have a life in Chicago. I understand. But none of it means we can't have a little fun while you're here, though, right? I like spending time with you. I know the ground rules. I'm okay with them. I just want to make the most of the time we do have. Unless it isn't what you want."

"No, I do." Lana breathed a sigh of relief. "I only wanted to lay all my cards out on the table. To let you know where things stand."

She leaned in and touched her lips to Court's, lingering

far longer than she'd meant to. Before she knew what was happening, she'd pushed Court onto her back and was stretched out on top of her, their tongues dueling for control. Court's hands were in her hair and she was reaching between them trying to unbutton Court's jeans when she heard the front door open. She moved so fast to get off Court she ended up on the floor in front of the couch. Court sat up and looked behind her to the door.

"Lori, hey," she said, and Lana wanted nothing more than to crawl under the couch and hide. Forever, if necessary. "You're home early."

"Yeah, he was an idiot," she said. "Story of my life."

The door slammed shut and Lana heard heels walking across the floor, but thankfully they receded as Lori went right into the kitchen. Court glanced down at her and mouthed *sorry* before jumping up and heading there after her. Lana took the opportunity to scramble back to her seat and did her best to straighten her hair just as they returned from the kitchen.

"Shit, did I interrupt something?" Lori asked, looking back and forth between the two of them. "I'm sorry."

"Nothing to apologize for," Lana said as she got to her feet. "We just took the kids up to bed a little while ago, and I was about to leave."

"Not because of me?" Lori held a hand out and began to walk backward toward the stairs. "I can get the kids and go home."

"No, really, I have to pick up my son from work." Lana hurried to put on her coat and Court walked with her to the door. "It was nice to see you again."

Court closed the door behind them and Lana finally let out a sigh of relief when she turned back to look at her.

"You don't have to go," Court said.

"I do. I'll call you, okay?"

"Can I see you Saturday? We have a game, but maybe after?"

"I'll be working. Come by for a slice if you feel like it."

She turned before Court could kiss her good-bye. She didn't look back because she feared if she did, she'd change her mind and stay.

CHAPTER NINETEEN

Tell me what your biggest problem with passing is," Court said to Eric when they were both on the ice Saturday morning. They had a little over an hour before her team would arrive for their morning skate. They were dressed in full pads and both had sticks in their hands.

"I just don't do it. I mean, when we have a play set up in the offensive zone I can," he answered with a shrug. "But when I'm skating up the ice, all I can think is shoot. Passing to someone else doesn't even cross my mind."

"Okay." Court looked toward the goal at the other end of the ice and skated to the bench for a puck. She dropped it and floated a pass to him, which he easily controlled with his stick. "We're going to skate toward the net, and I want you to pass it to me before we get there."

He nodded his agreement and they both took off. Court slowed down and let him go, wanting to see if he was going to look for her. He didn't. He shot the puck into the net and skated back to her.

"Is that how you always do it?"

"What do you mean?"

"You never took your eyes off the puck," she said. "You didn't even look to see where I was."

"I knew I had the better angle."

"Really? Eric, there's no goalie. There was no *angle*. We need to work on your vision. You need to know where your teammates are at any given time." Court watched him for a moment, taking mental notes as to his reactions to what she was telling him. "How many goals did you score last season?"

"Forty-two," he answered.

"How many assists?"

"Seventeen."

"And how many of those assists were from a direct pass, and how many of them were just an accident because you happened to touch the puck before a pass was made to the guy who scored the goal?"

He shrugged and Court sighed. She didn't know what she'd expected from these training sessions with him, but she didn't think he'd be a complete puck hog. She skated to the goal to retrieve the puck and brought it back to him.

"How many games did you play to get those fifty-nine points?" she asked when she stopped in front of him.

"Thirty-two."

"Impressive. But you know, all the best players get more assists than goals," she said, skating around him while maneuvering the puck between his feet and her own as she went. He was turning in circles watching her. "You want to make it to the NHL?"

"Of course I do," he said.

"Then you need to learn how to see the entire ice surface, not just the narrow strip of land in front of you." She went to one end of the ice and motioned for him to follow. They stood to the side of the net and she picked the puck up. "Follow me up the ice. I don't care where you are behind me—right, left, whatever. Just *stay* behind me somewhere."

He nodded and she tossed the puck ahead before taking off after it. After crossing the line into the opposite zone, she dropped the puck back, right onto his stick. He shot it into the net and skated to her.

"How did you know where I was?" he asked, the amazement evident in his expression and his tone. "You put it right on my stick."

"It wasn't hard, Eric. We're the only two in the building." She grinned, pleased that she'd impressed him. "When you do attempt a pass, you're probably doing it based solely on the play the coach has mapped out, am I right?"

"Yeah." He sounded like the answer should have been obvious to her. Unfortunately, it was, which was where his biggest problem lay.

"You can have set plays, and you can practice them until you're blue in the face," she said, keeping eye contact as she spoke. "But none of it matters. Because the fact is, you never know how the other team is going to react to every little move you make. And once they see you do the same thing over and over, they know exactly where they need to be in order to break up your play. Your vision of the ice isn't only about what you can see. You need to let your other senses take over. Listen for the cues from your teammates. Take quick glances away from the puck to see how things are developing in front of you, and listen to your gut when things fall apart."

They worked for a while longer, until the first of the Warriors made their way onto the ice. Court wanted to see him actually play in a game, because she knew seeing him in action would tell her what she needed to really help him work on. She skated with him to the gate leading off the ice.

"Thanks for helping." He stepped off and turned to face her. "My first game is Tuesday. I was wondering if you might want to come watch."

"I'd love to," she said, smiling at him. "And if you're free Thursday afternoon, maybe we can work a little more."

"That would be great." He nodded once before turning and heading for the locker room to change out of his uniform.

"Court," she heard from the ice behind her. She turned to see Gail skating toward her. "Who was that?"

"Eric. Lana's son," she said before taking a couple of strides to join her teammates. Gail grabbed the arm of her jersey to stop her. Court sighed.

"You're coaching him?" she asked, sounding surprised.

"Is that a problem?"

"No, I think it's great. I've always told you I thought you'd be a great coach when your playing days were over." Gail let go of her but she stayed where she was. "Are things serious between you and Lana?"

"No," was all Court said in response.

"Are you sleeping with her?"

"Excuse me?" Court didn't see how it was any of her business.

"Hey, chill out, okay? I'm asking as a friend. You never had a problem talking about women with me before."

Court glanced down at her skates, feeling like an idiot. Of course she always talked with Gail about her personal life. Gail was her best friend. Who else could she talk to about it?

"I'm sorry," she said. "You're right. She did spend the night with me on Thursday."

"But it's not serious?"

"It can't be, Gail. Her home is in Chicago. My home is here." Court wasn't entirely sure she'd want it to be serious even if the situation were different. It wasn't like she'd ever been able to make a relationship work anyway. Maybe it was better if the time with Lana had a strict expiration date.

"I'm not sure I believe you're okay with that," Gail said. Court tried to argue with her, but Gail raised her hand as she skated away, speaking over her shoulder. "I know you, Court. Sometimes I think I might know you better than you know yourself."

Court stared after her, but she had to laugh at herself. She knew Gail was right. Court could tell herself she was okay with the arrangement she'd made with Lana, but she also knew she was already starting to feel more than she should. Not only for Lana, but for Eric too. And it scared the hell out of her.

CHAPTER TWENTY

The next six weeks flew by for Court, and before she knew it, Thanksgiving was only a few days away. She and Lana spent a lot of time together, and things were going great between them as far as Court was concerned. Finding time to be alone proved to be difficult at times, but they managed somehow. They'd fallen into a routine where Eric worked every Friday night and then spent the night at his grandparents' house. Then on Saturdays Court and Lana would pick him up to take him to his hockey game.

Court even had a tense unspoken agreement with Jen Hilton that they'd stay out of each other's way. And it truly was unspoken—they didn't speak. At all. The arrangement worked just fine for Court. It seemed to be working great for the team as well. They were on top of their division and had only lost five games out of their first thirty.

"What are you doing for Thanksgiving?" Court asked that Saturday morning after Lana served her breakfast in bed. They were spending their last few moments together in each other's arms before having to get ready to pick Eric up for his game.

"Nothing like waiting until the last minute," Lana said,

tickling her side and causing Court to squirm as they both laughed. "My dad will be coming home on Tuesday, so Mom is planning on making her usual feast. When I was little we never celebrated it, because, well, my grandparents came from Italy. Joey and I bitched and moaned about how our friends always had these big dinners with turkey and everything, so they finally gave in and started to do it for us."

"That's nice," Court said, pulling her tighter against her body. She sighed and closed her eyes. This was only the fifth Thanksgiving since her father died, and it was still difficult for her to get into the spirit of turkey day. She did it for Ryan and Alice, but it was hard for both her and Lori.

"Why do you ask?" Lana said, leaning back slightly to see her face.

"I was going to invite you and Eric to Lori's if you didn't have plans."

"You're so sweet," Lana said, pressing her lips softly against Court's.

"Just don't spread it around," Court said. "I have a reputation to uphold, and being sweet would ruin everything."

"Your secret's safe with me, Courtney Court."

"I like it when you call me that," Court said with a grin. "I don't know why, but I do."

"You know what I like?" Lana asked. Court shook her head, so Lana took her by the wrist and moved her hand between her legs, moaning when Court's fingers slid through her wet folds. "I *really* like it when you touch me."

"Fuck," Court whispered into her ear, her own arousal ratcheting up a notch or three.

"Mmm," Lana said. "I like that too."

"Good," Court said as she moved to settle between Lana's legs. "We have something in common, then."

Forty-five minutes later, they were rushing to get out the door so they wouldn't be late getting Eric to the arena. They took their seats and settled in to wait for the game to start. They weren't there even five minutes before a man came and sat next to Court. He looked familiar to her, but she couldn't place where she knew him from.

"Courtney Abbott?" he asked and held his hand out to her.

"Yeah," she said, eyeing him suspiciously as she shook his hand.

"My name is Sid Clay."

"You're a scout." Court knew his name. She'd never met him, but she'd seen him in photos on the Canadian Hockey League website. She glanced at Lana, who seemed interested in their conversation. "This is Lana Caruso."

"Caruso," he said with a nod. "I'm here to see Eric play. Are you his mother?"

"Yes," Lana said, sounding wary.

"How did you hear about him?" Court asked. Clay's reputation was a good one, and Court was thrilled for Eric because someone of Clay's caliber was scouting him.

"I have my sources." He laughed and moved to the bench in front of them so he could speak to them together. He looked at Lana. "I know he had scouts watching him in Chicago, and I'm sure he'd be happy to play for one of those teams, but they're minor league at best. Now that you're living in Pennsylvania, he's eligible for the Quebec Major Junior Hockey League draft coming up in April. His chances of moving on to the NHL are infinitely better playing for us."

"Our permanent address is in Chicago," Lana said, shaking her head.

"Doesn't matter. You're living here now, and he's playing here. When does he turn sixteen?"

"February."

"And will you still be living here in April?"

"Yes," Lana said. Court took her hand and squeezed it. She could tell Lana was a little overwhelmed and wanted her to know she was there for her. Lana squeezed her back.

"Then that's perfect." He reached into his pocket and pulled out a business card which he handed to Lana. "Feel free to call me if you ever have any questions about anything."

"Oh, all right." Lana took the card and looked it over. "Should I give you my number?"

"No need right now." He stood and shook her hand before grasping Court's again. "I know how to get in touch with his coach, and if I like what I see today, maybe I can catch up with you after the game."

Court watched him as he walked away, wondering why he'd introduced himself to her in the first place if he hadn't known Lana was Eric's mother.

"He seems a little full of himself, doesn't he?" Lana asked. Court saw her shove Clay's card into her back pocket.

"He's earned it," she told her. "He's scouted a lot of players who've ended up in the NHL."

"You really think he's interested in Eric?"

"I do." Court took her hand and held it lightly between both of hers. "He's improved so much since I first started working with him. I wouldn't be surprised to see him on a pro team in another four or five years."

Lana did her best to not act as excited as she felt. It was one thing to know there were smaller junior leagues interested in Eric, but she'd done her homework. The three leagues under the umbrella of the CHL were a huge source of draft picks for the NHL. If Eric could make it there, he'd be on his way.

The final buzzer sounded and Eric's team won seven to two. Eric scored a hat trick, and before Lana could even think about leaving her seat, Sid Clay was there to see them. She smiled at him, hoping he'd been impressed by Eric.

"He's definitely a talented kid," he said with a nod. "I have his stat sheet, so I know this game wasn't a fluke. Today isn't the only time I'll watch him either. I'll be here for the last game of the season, right before Christmas. And I have no doubt they'll win the championship if they continue to play like they did today. Your son could have a bright future ahead of him."

They talked while she and Court waited for Eric to shower and get dressed, and Lana did end up giving him her phone number. He assured her he'd be in touch as the draft approached to go over any details and answer any questions she might have.

"Should I tell him?" Lana asked when they saw Eric, his gear bag slung over his shoulder, emerge from the locker room.

"It's up to you," Court said with a shrug.

Lana nodded, but she couldn't shake the feeling she wanted Court to be involved in this. The truth was, she wanted Court involved with everything in her life, and the realization caused a queasy feeling in her gut. This wasn't supposed to be happening. She stood to the side as a small group of kids approached Court for her autograph.

She smiled as she watched them, Court being her gracious self and answering all the questions they could throw at her. Eric walked up to Lana and put his arm around her shoulders, dropping his bag to the ground beside him.

"They really love her," he said.

"They do." Lana nodded but never took her eyes off Court. *And I think I do too.* She gave herself a mental shake, trying to dispel the errant thought. It wasn't part of their arrangement. And Court would probably laugh at her if she were to tell her what she was feeling. She needed to remind herself every so often, or else she was sure she'd be in trouble.

It might be too late for that.

Chapter Twenty-one

"Mom!" Eric yelled as he entered the house, slamming the door behind him. It was Christmas Eve, and she didn't feel like yelling at him for the hundredth time about slamming doors. "Mom! Where are you?"

"In the kitchen," she said, looking at Court and shaking her head. Court grinned at her but said nothing. They both knew why he was so excited. Sid Clay had been at his last game and talked to Lana about possibly taking Eric in the upcoming draft. There were other teams looking at him too, but Sid was the only one who had taken the time to speak with Lana. She'd decided not to tell him about it, but the only thing he got this worked up about was hockey, so she knew someone spilled the beans to him.

He rounded the corner into the kitchen and his smile was bigger than she'd ever seen it before. He looked at them and shook his head, obviously able to tell they already knew.

"I don't need to tell you, do I?" he asked, but his smile never faltered.

"Tell me what?" Lana asked, trying to sound innocent.

"I'm probably getting drafted."

"Into the military?" Lana asked.

"Ha ha," he said. He shrugged out of his coat and hung it over the back of a kitchen chair. "You're a comedian. No, in the QMJHL draft. You already knew, didn't you?"

"Yes, honey, I did," she said, enveloping him in a hug. He had to bend over for her to do it, though. Not for the first time, she wondered when the hell he'd gotten so big. He was just over six feet tall and had to weigh close to two hundred pounds. He'd had a heck of a growth spurt in the past few months and had been working out with weights more. Frankly, she was having trouble keeping enough food in the house for him. "I'm so proud of you."

"I know I owe a lot of it to you," he said when she released him, directing his comment to Court. She stood and Lana smiled as she watched Eric hug her too. He was even taller than Court now. "Thank you for all your help."

"So that's it?" Court asked, winking at Lana over his shoulder. "You're done with me now?"

"No," he said, sounding serious. "Not even close."

He glanced over his shoulder at Lana, who looked away from both of them.

"Go get ready," she told him. "Your grandmother is expecting us for dinner soon."

"Are you coming with us?" he asked Court, who shook her head with a small smile.

He looked as though he had something else to say, but finally shook his head and left the room. Court sat once again and Lana could feel her eyes on her, almost like she was actually touching her. She hadn't let Court know Eric understood they were together, but she also knew Court wasn't stupid. It just wasn't something that ever came up in conversation.

"You're awfully quiet," Court said after a moment. "Is everything okay?"

"He knows we're sleeping together."

Court nodded, but said nothing. Lana saw the look she gave her and knew she was worried about what the revelation meant for them. She wanted to tell her nothing had changed, but she'd be lying. If Court thought it was because Eric found out, maybe it was for the best.

"I think maybe we should stop."

"Wait, what?" Court asked. Maybe Lana had misunderstood the look. "I know that isn't what you want, and neither do I. What's really going on?"

I'm falling in love with you.

God, how Lana wished she could say those words, but what would it accomplish? She wasn't about to give up her career to live in Kingsville, and she would never ask Court to give up hers and move to Chicago. Maybe it was better to end things now. Eric was growing too close to Court, and she knew it would hurt him more the longer she let this go on between them. Who was she kidding? It would hurt *her* more the longer she let it go on.

"You don't want to date a woman who has a kid, remember?" Lana asked, thinking if she pissed Court off she'd leave without her having to actually ask her to.

"He's not a kid," Court said, shaking her head. "He's a young man. A pretty awesome one, actually. What about the draft? You said you wanted me here for that."

"I do," Lana said, somewhat surprised at the stab of pain in her chest. "I don't want to lose you as a friend, but I think we're spending too much time together. I don't want Eric thinking this is going to be something that will last."

"Eric? Or you?" Court got to her feet so fast the chair she was sitting in fell backward. Lana could see both anger and hurt in her eyes. It was the pain she saw there that almost persuaded her to change her mind. Court pulled the keys out of her pocket and headed for the front door. "Merry Christmas."

Lana wanted to go after her, wanted to tell her she hadn't meant it, but she couldn't. A quick break would be better for them both, even if Court couldn't see it now. When the front door opened and then closed, Lana let out a shaky breath, but she refused to cry.

❖

"Seriously?" Lori asked after Court told her what Lana had said.

They'd had dinner and the kids were in bed. They were sitting on the couch watching *It's a Wonderful Life*—a Christmas Eve tradition that only served to make Court miss their father even more. She didn't mind the fact they were ignoring some of it while they were talking.

"Nice parting shot, by the way." Lori nudged her with her elbow, and Court allowed a small smile. "How did she respond?"

"She didn't say anything, so I left."

"She didn't try to stop you?"

Court shook her head. She'd been angry, but she'd taken her time walking to the car, and then again backing out of the driveway, just in case Lana wanted to stop her.

"It doesn't matter."

"The hell it doesn't," Lori said, turning to face her. "You're in love with her, Court. And," she added as she put her hand over Court's mouth when she tried to protest, "she's in love with you."

Court shook her head and pushed her hand away.

"No, she's not, and neither am I. We both agreed when this started it was temporary. Anything long-term would never work out."

"Bullshit," Lori said, crossing her arms over her chest.

"People have long-distance romances all the time. And whether you want to admit it or not, you won't be playing hockey forever."

"No, but I have another year on my contract, and the team has an option for another year after that." Court cringed at the thought of having to play with Jen Hilton for two more years, but she loved this team, and she loved the city. Not to mention Lori and the kids lived right next door. "This is my home."

"But it doesn't have to be your home forever, Court." Lori was exasperated, she could tell. "Don't you dare tell me the only reason you want to stay here is me and the kids. At the end of the day, we aren't your responsibility. Do I love having you next door? Absolutely. Will we miss you? Hell, yes, but you need to live your life for you, not for us."

"You aren't listening, Lori. *She* ended it, not me." Court stood to go. She just wanted to be alone, and her head was starting to ache. She rubbed her temples, her finger running across the scar under her eye. Lana was at the game when it happened. She'd likely never be at another game, and the realization threatened to rip Court apart. "I'm not going to beg her to continue something that would be over again in another few months."

"You are infuriating, do you know that?"

Court chose not to answer, figuring it was a rhetorical question anyway. She slipped her shoes on and grabbed her jacket.

"I'll see you in the morning?" Court asked. Lori just waved in her direction, a sure sign she wasn't happy with her.

CHAPTER TWENTY-TWO

How's your mother doing?" Court asked Eric a couple of weeks later when he showed up before her morning skate with the Warriors. He was sitting on the team bench waiting for her when she emerged from the locker room. She hadn't seen or heard from Lana or Eric since Christmas Eve, and she lost track of how many times she'd driven to the pizzeria only to leave again without going inside. "And you missed a couple of our sessions. A phone call would have been nice."

"She told me not to come anymore," Eric said, looking at his feet.

"Look at me when you're talking to me," she told him. It was something she'd instructed him to do while they were working together.

"She told me not to come anymore," he said again, meeting her eyes and sounding angrier than he had the first time he said it. "What did you do to her?"

"Nothing. She ended things, not me."

He stared at her; no doubt his mind was racing to try to reconcile what she'd said with whatever story his mother had given him. Court didn't have time for this. She turned to skate away from the boards, but his voice, full of hurt, stopped her in her tracks.

"She's miserable," he said. "Are you?"

"Eric, this really isn't any of your business, okay?" she said, trying to sound sympathetic, but not knowing if she was succeeding. His words gave her hope, but she'd learned long ago that hope was fleeting.

"My mother isn't my business?" he asked incredulously.

"No, that isn't what I mean," she said. She returned to the boards and lowered her voice when she saw the rest of her team coming onto the ice. "You guys are leaving in a few months. It was never going to last, Eric."

"So, what? You both just give up? God, adults are so ridiculous."

Court couldn't help but laugh, because she kind of agreed with him.

"Hey, Abbott, I haven't seen your girlfriend around lately," Jen Hilton called from a few feet away. Unfortunately, she'd been doing her best to get under Court's skin again. Court tried like hell to ignore her, but it was almost impossible. "You moved on to little boys now, pervert?"

Eric looked at her, but Court shook her head. It wasn't worth getting into it with her, and Court didn't want him starting anything.

"You're going to let her talk to you like that?" he asked. When Court just shook her head again, he looked across the ice toward Hilton. "Hey, bitch, come over here and say that."

"Eric, knock it off," she said under her breath. Too late. She heard Hilton come to a stop behind her, spraying ice on her and Eric in the process.

"Isn't this sweet," Hilton said. "You need a little boy to fight your battles."

"Shut the fuck up," Court said without turning around. She was still hoping she'd be able to defuse the situation, but the look on Eric's face told her it was too late. In fact, he started to climb over the boards so she placed a hand in the center of his chest and held him in place. She lowered her voice so Hilton couldn't hear her. "You really want to fight with a woman? I'm sure your mother would have both our heads if I let that happen."

After taking a deep breath, she finally turned and faced Hilton.

"Did your girlfriend dump you because she found out you liked little boys?" Hilton asked.

"I don't need anyone to fight my battles," Court said through clenched teeth. She didn't even pretend to give credence to her last comment. "Especially against someone like you."

"What the hell is that supposed to mean?" Hilton dropped her stick and gloves, but Court just shook her head and chuckled. "You're going to laugh at me?"

"Back off, Hilton," Court said, then glanced over her shoulder. "You need to leave now, Eric."

"But, Court—"

"Now!" Court ducked just as Hilton threw a punch. She didn't bother looking behind her again. She just hoped he was doing as she told him. She shoved Hilton in the shoulder, knocking her to the ice. Court hovered over her. "You'll stay down if you know what's good for you."

"Fuck you," Hilton said with a sneer. She got to her feet and tried to hit her again, but Court blocked the punch with her gloved hand. "Fight me, dyke."

"Is that supposed to be an insult?" Court asked. "I've heard much worse, and from far better people than you."

"You're an abomination, and an embarrassment to this team," Hilton said. She was so angry she was spitting while she spoke. "You're going to hell, you know that, right?"

"Seriously? Some days I feel like I'm already there," Court told her and couldn't help but laugh. It only made Hilton angrier. "I'm so sick of people using religion to justify their hate. If you want to hate me, then own it. Don't hide behind the church."

Court tried to skate away, but Hilton went after her. Court was expecting her to, and she was ready. She tossed her gloves and turned, all in one swift motion, and threw a right cross. It hit its mark, and as soon as her fist made contact with Hilton's jaw, Hilton crumpled to the ice.

"What the hell is going on?" Gail yelled as she and the rest of the team raced over.

Hilton bounced right up again and charged Court, grabbing her around the waist and taking them both down, Court on her back and Hilton on top of her.

"Why didn't you just tell me you were jealous, sweetheart?" Court said, keeping her voice low enough so only Hilton could hear her. Before Hilton could spew whatever hate-filled rant she was planning, she was pulled off Court by their teammates.

"You're both out." Gail looked back and forth between them as Savannah and Kelly helped Court to her feet. "You're not playing tonight. In fact, I don't even want to see either one of you in this building at all. Is that understood?"

"Coach," Court said, trying to explain, but Gail cut her off.

"I don't want to hear it. Keep talking, and I might just bench you for the rest of the year." Court had never seen Gail so pissed. She was actually red in the face. Court half expected to see steam coming from her ears. Gail focused her attention on Hilton then. "You get dressed and get the hell out of here. Now!"

The team backed away from Hilton and watched her skate off the ice. Court never took her eyes from Gail, but she knew exactly the moment when everyone turned their sights back to her.

"Coach," Court said, trying again to reason with her. Gail yelled at everyone to get to work, and Court waited for everyone to skate away before talking again. "Gail, she's been asking for it for weeks. You know that."

"I do, and I also thought I knew you were better than this. What the hell's been going on with you? You look ready to fight every time you step on the ice anymore." Gail waited for an answer, and Court shuffled her feet as she stared down at the ice.

Ever since Christmas Eve, Court had done her best to not be alone with Gail. She knew she'd have to tell her about how Lana ended things with her, and she really didn't want to get into it. If she hadn't had to be at Lori's the night it happened, she probably wouldn't have told her either.

"Nothing's going on," Court lied. "She just pushed me too far."

"Bullshit," Gail said, shaking her head. "Until you want to tell me what's happening, you're suspended. No practices, no games, no nothing. Understood?"

Court just stared at her for a moment, but finally nodded. Gail turned her back and skated away, and Court let out a breath. It was no use arguing with Gail in the heat of the moment, so she made the decision to call her later. She looked into the stands and was relieved to see Eric was gone.

❖

Court walked into Caruso's that evening at a little after six. Luckily, Lana was in the kitchen and hadn't seen her, so she walked to a table in the back and sat down. She watched Lana delivering food and drinks to the table next to hers, but Lana still hadn't seen her. Her heart skipped a beat when Lana headed her way and their eyes finally met. Court noticed the falter in her step, but to Lana's credit, she put on a smile and held up her order pad.

"What are you doing here?" she asked, sounding equal parts mad and surprised.

"It's a restaurant." Court shrugged. "It's dinnertime. I was hungry."

"You have a game in an hour."

"I'm not playing tonight."

"Why?"

"Can you sit down for a second?" Court asked, glancing around the dining area. It was busy, but it looked like everyone was eating at the moment. "We need to talk."

"Are you hurt?" Lana seemed concerned, and Court allowed herself to feel a little bit of hope. Lana slid into the booth across from her and set her order pad on the table. "Eric told me you got into a fight with Jen Hilton this morning."

"I'm fine. Gail benched us both for tonight."

"Eric told me what she said to you."

"That's why I'm here, actually," Court said. She rested her forearms on the table and leaned forward. She wanted nothing more than to take Lana's hand, but she resisted. "I don't need him to defend me."

"He cares about you, Court," Lana said, a flash of defiance in her eyes causing Court to flinch. "I've taught him to stand up for people who are being attacked. I won't tell him what he did was wrong."

"I'm sorry. You're absolutely right," she said, feeling like a bit of a heel. "My father raised me to stand up for myself. I've had teammates come to my aid during games, but I've never had someone defend me like that, outside of the confines of game play."

"From what he said, she was disparaging him as well. Is he not allowed to defend himself?" Lana grabbed her order pad and got to her feet, but pointed at her with her pen before walking away. "He did what any decent young man would do, and telling him otherwise would be taking a step backward."

Court sat there, her head in her hands for what felt like forever. It was obvious Lana wasn't going to take her order, so she decided to leave, but she intended to be waiting outside for her when she got off later. She'd hoped maybe they could start over, and this conversation hadn't gone at all as she'd expected.

Chapter Twenty-three

O h my God, she can be infuriating," Lana said when she returned to the kitchen. Joey stopped what he was doing and stared at her.

"Who are we talking about?" he asked.

"Who else? Courtney Abbott." Lana threw her pad at him and took off her apron. "I need a break."

"Greg, take over here," Joey said to his assistant. He took Lana by the elbow and led her into the office. Once they were seated, he tried to get her to tell him what was going on.

He knew Lana had ended things with Court, but he also knew she was regretting the decision. He also knew Eric was going through a tough time because of it. Lana really didn't want to talk about this with him, but he'd obviously been holding his tongue as long as he could.

"Did you ever think maybe in the process of protecting your own heart, you might have broken hers?" he asked after she'd relayed the events of the day.

"Whose side are you on?" she asked, feeling attacked.

"Seriously?" He looked hurt, but Lana didn't feel like placating him at the moment. "I'm not on anyone's side. I just want my sister to be happy. And whether you want to believe it or not, you were happy when you were with her. The past couple of weeks...not so much."

"She was fine with the arrangement we had," Lana said, not wanting to think too much about it. If she thought about it, she might feel the need to do something about it, and she felt what she'd done was the best thing for both of them. Nothing Joey said could change her mind.

"You really think she only came here tonight to ask you to stop Eric from standing up for her? Don't you think she can fight her own battles?"

"Of course she can, which is why she wants Eric to back off." Lana sighed. It wasn't going to be easy to not see Court for the next four months, but it was what she had to do. Not only to protect her heart, but to keep from wanting to devour her every time she saw her. "This really isn't any of your business, Joey."

"The hell it isn't," he said. "You haven't been yourself lately, Lana. You're abrupt with the customers, and you screw up orders on a regular basis. I need someone who can keep their head in the game."

"Are you firing me?" Not that he really could, since he wasn't even paying her to work, but the thought of it still pissed her off. "Seriously?"

"I'm not firing you," he said, his exasperation obvious by the way he pushed back from his desk. He marched to the door but stopped, his hand resting on the knob. "I just want my sister back. And I'm pretty sure Eric would like his mother back."

Lana stared at the door after he left, and for a moment, her resolve wavered. Would it really hurt anything to continue seeing Court for the next few months? She had to admit she'd been happier before she ended it. She shook her head. No, it would be better to keep things as they were now. By the time they went back to Chicago, maybe the pain in her chest would be gone.

❖

Lana walked out the back door of the restaurant when her shift was over and took a deep breath. She took her phone out and scrolled to Court's name. It wasn't the first time she'd done it this evening, and as before, she turned it off and shoved it back into her pocket.

"There's no reason to call her," she murmured as she dug her keys out. She wouldn't even know what to say. It was obvious Court was okay with ending things because she hadn't said anything about it when she was there earlier. She fought the urge to pull the phone back out. "It's better this way."

Her phone rang then, and she jumped a little, placing her hand on her chest. Court's name was displayed and she couldn't stop the feeling of happiness surging through her. Really? Just because of a name on her phone? She was pathetic.

"Hello," she said as she walked toward her car. She tried to sound less excited than she felt at the prospect of hearing Court's voice.

"Hey," Court said.

Lana stopped in her tracks, surprised Court's voice wasn't only in her ear. She turned and saw her standing a few feet away, just around the corner of the building where Lana hadn't been able to see her when she'd first walked out.

"I miss you, Lana," she said into the phone as she took a tentative step toward her. "Can we talk?"

Lana found herself nodding as she shut off her phone. She didn't move while Court closed the remaining distance between them. She looked so unsure of herself standing there before her, Lana wanted to pull her closer. Instead, she placed a hand on the center of Court's chest, just below her collarbone.

"I miss you too," she said, all resolve flying out the window while Court was right there where she could touch her.

"Can we start over?" Court asked, covering her hand with her own. "Please?"

It was in that moment Lana realized she was powerless to deny Court anything. How stupid of her to think she could have refused to accept the feelings she was having for Court.

"Yes," Lana said. She moved her hand so it was behind her neck and pulled Court in for a kiss. Just a quick one, but it didn't prevent the sparks between them.

"Come home with me."

"I can't," Lana said. She placed a hand on Court's cheek and shook her head. "Eric's at home tonight."

The disappointment from Court was palpable, and Lana scrambled to reassure her this wasn't a rejection.

"Why don't you come home with me?" she asked before she could really think about what she was asking.

"What about Eric?" Court asked.

Lana smiled and patted her cheek. "I didn't say you were going to spend the night."

"You didn't say I wouldn't be spending the night either," Court said with a wink.

"No, I didn't." Lana shook her head. "But if we're starting over, I wouldn't be counting on it, if I were you."

Court agreed to meet her at her house, and Lana took

the time alone during the drive to wonder if she was doing the right thing. She had to admit Joey had been right about one thing. She was much happier with Court in her life. She simply needed to remind herself every so often this was only a temporary situation.

Only it wasn't so simple, was it? She was falling for Court, and she felt helpless to stop it. She didn't want to admit she had no desire to stop it. The path she was going down would only lead to disappointment in the end, but she had a feeling the trip getting there was something she wouldn't want to miss. As far as she was concerned, Court was worth it.

She didn't want to think too much about the future. For the first time in her life, she wanted to live in the moment. It was a scary concept, but she was determined to do it.

Court wasn't there yet when she arrived, so she went into the house, intending to give Eric a heads-up about their impending visitor. She was surprised when she walked in and found him in the living room. On the couch with a girl. A girl she'd never met before. She was grateful they were sitting on opposite ends of the couch, and their attention was focused on the television.

"Eric?' she said as she hung up her coat. "Are you going to introduce me to your friend?"

"Mom, you're home early," he said, jumping to his feet as if he were feeling guilty about something. He looked at the girl and then back to her. "This is Angie. We were just watching a movie."

"Hello, Angie," she said with a smile.

"Hi, Mrs. Caruso," Angie replied. Lana didn't feel the need to correct the girl's assumption she was married. She'd always left it up to Eric to tell his friends if he chose to. "I should probably go, Eric."

They said good-bye, and Eric walked her out to her car,

which was apparently parked on the street since Lana hadn't noticed it when she pulled in. She wasn't sure she was happy if Eric had a girlfriend with a car. And not only because it meant she was older than him.

"My little boy is definitely growing up."

CHAPTER TWENTY-FOUR

Court stopped outside the front door, realizing she was more nervous now than she had been when she'd shown up for the dinner Eric had arranged for her and Lana. Her heart felt as if it were going to beat right out of her chest. She took a deep breath and closed her eyes briefly before knocking on the door.

"I'll get it!" she heard Eric call from inside.

"We aren't finished with this conversation," Lana said as he opened the door. Court found herself standing face-to-face with Eric, and he didn't appear to be happy to see her.

"What are you doing here?" he asked, not budging from where he stood.

"Eric, let her in," Lana said, pulling him out of the way so Court could walk in. Lana shut the door and Court looked at him again.

"I owe you an apology," Court said to him. His expression seemed to soften a bit, but she could tell he wasn't completely convinced. She glanced at Lana. "I owe you both an apology. Eric, I'm not used to anyone standing up for me. Your mother pointed out that Hilton was pushing both of us, but I couldn't see it in the moment. She's been trying to goad me into a fight since the first day she stepped on the ice with me, and today she finally pushed me too far. I'm sorry I snapped at you. And I want to thank you for trying to come to my defense."

Eric held her gaze as she spoke, but when she finished, he looked down at his feet. After a moment, he glanced at Lana and then stood up straight and looked at Court once again, his hand out for her to shake.

"You're welcome, and I accept your apology," he said. Court looked at his hand and laughed as she pushed it away before pulling him into a hug. He stiffened for the briefest of moments, but then he hugged her back. He spoke into her ear low enough so Lana couldn't hear. "But if you ever hurt my mother, you'll have to answer to me."

She stepped back and nodded her silent acceptance of his warning. She had no intention of ever hurting her, but she knew if she did, she'd be in serious trouble. But she also knew no matter what happened between the two of them, Lana would always have someone watching her back. She smiled at Lana, who took her hand and laced their fingers together. Something in her world shifted, and Court felt like everything was right again.

"Why don't you go to your room, Eric," Lana said. She led Court into the living room, but Eric was right behind them.

"I will, but I want to hear her apology to you too." He took a seat in the chair across from the couch and watched them as they sat next to each other.

"I don't think—"

"It's okay," Court said, cutting her off. "He has the right to hear this too."

"Okay," Lana said, but she looked skeptical. "But you don't really owe me an apology. I owe you one. The only reason I ended things with you was because I thought we were spending too much time together. I didn't want anyone to start feeling more than they should."

"And I accused you of exactly that, so I am sorry." Court looked away, not wanting Lana to see in her eyes how much she was feeling. If she knew Court was falling for her, there'd be no way she'd want to start things over with her. Lana squeezed her hand, causing Court to look at her again.

"I'm sorry too." Lana gave a small smile and tilted her head. "I need to remember we're both adults, and neither one of us needs to look out for the other one. We both know where things stand, right?"

"Absolutely," Court answered, hoping she didn't answer too quickly.

"Okay, well, you guys are boring," Eric said with a grin as he stood. "I'm going to bed."

When he was gone, Court finally allowed herself to relax some. Lana went to the kitchen to get them each a beer, and Court glanced around the room. She felt a pang of disappointment because she'd missed out on Christmas with Lana and Eric. The last time she'd been here the decorations were still up. The tree was gone now, and the furniture was put back the way it had been before Christmas.

"Here you go," Lana said, handing her a bottle.

"I really have missed you, Lana," she said. Sitting so close to her didn't make it easy to keep her hands to herself, but she was determined to not push things. If they were going to go back to the way they were before, it would be up to Lana.

"I missed you too," Lana said, touching Court's cheek with her fingertips. "I just didn't realize how much until you showed up at Caruso's tonight."

"Eric said you were miserable," Court said with a grin.

"Eric exaggerates."

"Really? Because I don't mind admitting I was pretty miserable myself." Court shifted slightly so she was facing her, and she reached out to run her fingers through Lana's hair. Lana closed her eyes and leaned into her touch. "I didn't realize how much I enjoyed spending time with you until you weren't there anymore. And I didn't have a clue how I was going to avoid running into you for the next four months."

"I was having the same problem," Lana admitted with a sigh. "It wasn't the same listening to your games on the radio knowing I wouldn't be seeing you afterward."

"I'm glad I took the chance to see you tonight."

"Me too," Lana said, and she couldn't help herself. She leaned closer and pressed her lips to Court's. She resisted deepening the kiss, but when she pulled back, she saw her own desire reflected in Court's beautiful blue eyes. There was a storm brewing there, and it was all Lana could do to keep from ripping her clothes off right there on the couch. "I really missed this too."

"I should go," Court said, trying to extricate herself from Lana, but Lana held tight to her. "Unless you want your son to walk in on us here on the couch."

"No, that would be bad." Lana stood and pulled Court with her. "So I think we should go to my room."

"Are you sure?" Court looked nervous as she glanced down the hall where Eric's room was. Lana thought she looked adorable.

"He's not a child," Lana told her. She began walking toward the other end of the house pulling Court along with her. "And he already knows we've spent the night together before, so yeah, I'm sure. Unless you don't want to stay."

Court stopped walking and pulled on Lana's hand until she turned and Court pressed her body against hers. Lana's arms went around Court's neck.

"Do you doubt I want to be here with you?"

"No, I can see in your eyes how much you *do* want to be here." Lana smiled when she felt Court's hands move across her hips and down to cup her ass. "Not here, exactly, but maybe in my bed. Naked."

"You never told me you were a mind reader," Court said. She picked her up and Lana wrapped her legs around her waist.

"I need to have some secrets, don't I?"

"I suppose a little bit of mystery can be a good thing."

Lana held onto her like she never wanted to let her go as Court carried her into the bedroom, kicking the door closed behind them.

❖

Court slowly came awake when the aroma of cooking bacon reached her nose. She smiled and stretched, surprised to find Lana was still in bed with her, curled up along her side. She rolled over to face her, brushing the hair away from her eyes before pressing her lips to Lana's forehead. Lana stirred and moaned as she threw an arm over Court and opened her eyes.

"I like waking up with you," she mumbled.

"I thought you were already awake."

"What?" Lana raised up on an elbow and squinted down at her.

"You didn't start breakfast?" Court started to panic. She'd fully intended to be up and gone before Eric was awake, but it looked now like she'd missed her opportunity.

"Oh, shit," Lana said, looking wide-awake now. She threw the covers back and jumped out of bed, searching frantically for something to put on. "Shit, shit, shit."

"I knew I should have gone home last night," Court said, following suit. She pulled her jeans on and reached for the T-shirt she'd tossed on the floor the night before. "He's going to be pissed, isn't he?"

"Wait, what?" Lana asked, grabbing Court's arm and pulling her around to face her. "Eric is going to be fine with you still being here, I'm sure. My parents, on the other hand..."

"What?" Court said, her voice cracking. "Your parents? Here?"

"They'll be here soon," Lana said with a quick glance at the clock on her bedside table. "I can't believe I forgot they were coming for breakfast this morning."

"I should get out of here before they arrive," Court said, trying to put her shirt on, which was a little difficult since Lana wasn't letting go of her arm.

"No, it would look so much worse if you were doing the walk of shame." Lana stared at her, looking as though she were a deer caught in the headlights. Court pulled her into an embrace. "If you're already here, it will just seem like you came over for breakfast."

"You said you came out to them years ago, right?" Court asked, trying to rack her brain to remember what Lana had told her.

"Yes, and they've never been happy about it. I've never introduced them to anyone before." Lana pulled away so they could both finish getting dressed.

"Don't worry," Court said, attempting to lighten the mood. "Parents love me."

"Please don't take this the wrong way, but for them, you're just a friend, okay?" Lana's look pleaded with Court, and all Court could do was nod. She'd do anything for Lana.

"Yeah, okay," she said.

"Thank you." Lana gave her a quick kiss on the lips before rushing to the bathroom to try to tame her hair. "I promise I'll make it up to you."

Court grinned, thinking of all the ways she could accomplish that. After a moment, she hurried to follow Lana, knowing she had sex hair as well. There was no way anyone would believe she just dropped in for breakfast with her hair looking like it did.

Chapter Twenty-five

Court watched in amusement as Lana listened at the door and finally determined her parents weren't there yet. She shoved Court out of the bedroom and told her she'd be right behind her. Court started walking down the hall, but then found herself wondering how she was going to face Eric on her own. She stopped and turned back toward the bedroom, but Lana had closed the door again.

"You can do this," she whispered to herself. She took a deep breath and walked the remaining distance to the kitchen. Eric had his back to her, and she watched him for a moment as he cooked. "Good morning."

"Hey," he said, turning to face her. He grinned at her, and she felt her face heat up, knowing he knew exactly why she was still there this morning. "I take it you slept well?"

"You don't seem surprised to see me."

"I'm not," he said with a shrug. He turned back to the stove and removed the pan with the bacon in it. "Your car is still in the driveway, and you weren't on the couch, so I assumed you were with my mom."

"She's a mind reader, and you're a detective," Court said, amused.

"What?"

"Nothing." She pulled a chair out from the table and took a seat to watch him. "Do you cook a lot?"

"Just breakfast on Sundays," he answered, coming to sit with her. She noticed he appeared to be a little nervous now too. "Listen, you know my grandparents are coming, right?"

"Yeah, your mother told me."

"And she's okay with you being here?"

Court was wondering how to answer when Lana walked into the kitchen and saved her.

"I figured it was better for her to be here than for them to pull in while she's walking out of the house," Lana said. She went to the coffee pot and poured herself a cup. Court watched her as she grabbed a second cup and filled it too before coming and sitting with them.

"Ah," Eric said with a nod and a knowing smile. "The walk of shame."

"Excuse me?" Lana asked, her mouth dropping open. "What do you know about it?"

"I don't know, movies maybe?" he laughed. "Relax, Mom. I don't know about it from experience."

"Good."

Court jumped when the doorbell rang. Lana grabbed her hand and gave it a quick squeeze and a reassuring smile when Court looked at her. Court didn't move as Lana went to answer the door, wondering briefly if she had the time to sneak out the back door.

"Whose car is in the driveway, dear?" Lana's mother asked.

"Yeah, sis, whose car is out there?" Joey gave her a grin and a wink as she hung up everyone's coats.

Lana was still shocked every time she saw how frail her father looked. He'd been a strong man while she was growing up, and to see him sick and gaunt like this was a little heartbreaking to her. She backhanded Joey in the gut as she led them all into the kitchen.

"Mom, Dad, this is a friend of mine, Courtney Abbott," Lana said, noticing the look of distaste on her mother's face. Her father however, surprised her.

"Courtney Abbott? The hockey player?" he asked. He walked over to her and held his hand out, which Court took without hesitation. He looked at Joey. "Isn't she the one you wanted to do our commercial?"

"It's nice to meet you, sir," Court said with what looked to Lana to be an uncomfortable smile. Court looked at her mother and nodded once. "And you too, ma'am."

"You follow hockey?" Lana asked her father, a little surprised he knew who Court was.

"Who in this town doesn't know Courtney Abbott?" he asked with a shrug. He turned to Court then. "Call me Tony, please."

"Okay, Tony," Court said, sounding amused. "You can call me Court. And I'm sorry, but what was that you mentioned about a commercial?"

Lana went to help Eric finish with the breakfast while Joey and her mother went to join Court and her father at the table.

"Your *friend*?" Eric asked, nudging her in the ribs.

"Don't judge me," she said as she cracked open an egg.

"Grandpa seems taken with her."

Lana looked over her shoulder toward the table and was happy to see Court laughing at something her father said. One of his jokes, no doubt. She shook her head.

"Yeah, he does."

"Grandma seems wary, though."

"Because she doesn't believe Court's just a friend. She's suspicious by nature."

"I'm happy you and Court worked things out," he said after a few moments of silence. "I really like her."

"So do I," Lana said with a sigh. *Maybe too much.*

❖

After breakfast, Court insisted on helping Eric with the dishes, so Lana went to the living room with her parents and Joey. Now that they were away from Court, her mother apparently couldn't wait to get right to it.

"She's a friend, you said?"

"Yes, Mother," Lana answered, knowing this was coming but having hoped it would be another day rather than right this minute.

"How good a friend?" The look her mother gave her let her know she already knew the answer to the question, but she was challenging Lana to lie to her about it. Luckily, her father saved her from having to, much to Lana's surprise.

"Maria, stop," he said, a hand waving in the air. "What Lana does in the privacy of her own home is none of your business."

"But—"

"But nothing," he said. "Does she ask us about our sex life?"

Lana watched in horror as her mother's face turned an alarming shade of red. She almost burst out laughing when Joey snickered next to her. Instead she slapped his thigh and gave him her best dirty look.

"Tony," her mother said in admonishment.

"What?" he asked. He turned his attention to Lana and smiled as he reached for her hand. "I like her, Lana. You could do a lot worse."

"Thank you, Daddy," she managed to say around the lump

in her throat. She hadn't called him that since she'd been about ten years old. The tear he wiped from his eye let her know he was well aware of the fact also.

"I'm proud of the woman you've become," he said quietly. "And you've raised a good son. Or should I say a good young man. You should be proud of him."

"I am, thank you," she said, not trusting herself to say any more. Joey took her hand and smiled at her. It wasn't lost on Lana that Joey had been right when he told her their father seemed to be coming around. She smiled at Joey too. "And thank you."

CHAPTER TWENTY-SIX

April came fast. The Warriors were in the playoffs for the eighth consecutive year, and Court was playing better than she had during her Olympic years. Jen Hilton stayed out of her way, and Court had to admit Hilton's game play had improved, as had her attitude.

Eric was excited for the draft and had talked of little else for the three weeks leading up to it. Lana's entire family was gathered at her house for the event, which took place over the internet. Nothing flashy like the NHL or NFL drafts held every year, but it didn't seem to bother anyone.

Eric was sitting on the couch with the laptop on the coffee table in front of him, looking for all the world like he was going to jump right out of his skin. Court took a seat next to him and put her arm around his shoulders.

"Have you eaten anything?" she asked.

"I can't." He sat back and placed a hand over his stomach as he grimaced. "I think I'd just throw it up again."

Court laughed and clapped him on the back. She knew what he was feeling. Not on the same scale, of course, because while she'd always hoped to someday make it to the pros, she'd always known in the back of her mind it would never happen. But she remembered waiting on the edge of her seat for the call from Team USA to let her know whether or not she'd made the team the first time.

At Christmas, Eric had been sure he was going to go early in the draft. During the time when she and Lana weren't seeing each other anymore though, his play had suffered as he'd let his mother's misery rest squarely on his shoulders. His team didn't win a single game in the playoffs, and he'd been benched for his poor play. As a result, his stock in the draft dropped sharply.

"You'll be fine, Eric," she told him. "Even if, for some reason, you don't get drafted today, you'll still be fine. You know that, right? You're talented, and you're only sixteen. You can still sign with a team without being drafted too."

"Yeah, I know." He spared a quick glance her way, obviously not wanting to take his eyes off the computer screen for long even though the draft wouldn't start for another ten minutes. "Mom already told me all of that. But thanks. It means a lot coming from you."

She squeezed his shoulder before standing to go find Lana in the kitchen. She was getting chips and crackers and other snack items for everyone to munch on as they waited for Eric's name to be called. Or not.

"Hey," Court said as she took a seat at the table.

"Hey." Lana gave her a genuine smile, and it warmed Court's heart. She didn't think she'd ever get tired of having Lana smile at her like that. "Thank you for being here today."

"There's nowhere I'd rather be," Court assured her. Lana's family was in the living room, but Court found herself wishing they were alone in the house. In fact, she'd found herself wanting to be alone with Lana quite often lately, and although she knew she should be trying to slow things down in anticipation of Lana's impending departure, she had no desire to do it.

Lana pressed a hand to her stomach and shook her head, looking a lot like Eric had a few minutes earlier. "I'm so nervous for him. He's going to be devastated if he doesn't get drafted."

Court went to her and pulled her into a hug. Lana's arms went around her waist and she rested her head on Court's shoulder.

"He'll be fine, and so will you," she said, smoothing her hands along Lana's back and pressing a kiss to her temple. "It wouldn't be the end of the world if he doesn't get picked today, you know."

"Easy for you to say." Lana chuckled but didn't let go. "You won't have to deal with him all summer if he doesn't get drafted."

Court tried not to react to her words, but it was obvious Lana had felt something shift in her body language. She leaned back in Court's arms and searched her eyes.

"Don't go quiet on me now, Courtney Court. Tell me what you're thinking."

"I'm thinking I don't want you to go." Court swallowed hard and tried to pull away from her, but Lana refused to let go. She looked away, not wanting Lana to see what she knew she couldn't hide for much longer. Court was in love with her, and she wanted Lana to change her mind about moving back to Chicago. But she knew she could never ask that of her. She shook her head. "Totally selfish of me, I know. Forget I said anything."

"Hey," Lana said, cupping her chin and forcing Court to look at her. She gave her a sad smile, and Court returned it. "I can't forget it. I don't think I'll ever forget anything about you,

Court. You've touched a place in me I didn't know existed. Because of you, I know now that I can make a relationship work."

"Just not with me, right?" Court asked, immediately regretting the words *and* her tone of voice. She sounded like a whiny little bitch, and she hated herself for it. Lana pulled away from her then and leaned against the counter, her arms crossed over her chest as she stared at her. "I'm sorry. I didn't mean that."

"I think you did," Lana said with a nod. "Why are you doing this, Court? We talked about it from the beginning. You knew I'd be leaving. You can't ask me to stay."

"I'm not, Lana, but does that mean I can't even say I want you to?" Court asked. When Lana simply continued to stare, Court sighed and leaned against the counter too. "I said I knew it was selfish, but I was feeling it, so I said it. I know you're leaving. Believe me, the thought's never left my mind. It doesn't mean I can't want things to be different."

"If I didn't have a position I worked long and hard for waiting for me back in Chicago, maybe things could be different. But you know, it's not like there's another orchestra here I could join." Lana shook her head, and Court had the distinct feeling she'd had this argument before. Maybe with her brother? Or perhaps her mother? Or maybe just with herself. "I'll be leaving in a few weeks. Maybe it's time to put the brakes on here."

"That's not what I want," Court said, shaking her head. She wasn't above begging, but she knew instinctually Lana wouldn't respond well to it, so she refrained.

"I don't either, but I don't want saying good-bye to be any harder than it's going to be already," Lana said. Court thought she saw sadness in her eyes, but figured she was only seeing what she wanted to see.

"It won't be, I promise. I only have you for a few more weeks." Court took a chance and reached out for her hand. Lana took it and allowed Court to pull her into another hug. "I don't want to waste any of it."

"Lana," said her mother as she entered the kitchen. Lana pulled away and Court let her go. They both looked at Maria, who had stopped short when she saw their embrace. She looked between the two of them and shook her head. "It's about to start."

"Thanks, Mom," Lana said.

"Are you still going to try to convince me you're just *friends*?" Maria asked. Court cleared her throat to try to hide her grin. Maria's smirk didn't look to her like disapproval. It seemed more like amusement. "You must think I'm an old fool."

"That went well," Court said when Maria turned and walked back out to the living room. Lana backhanded her in the gut and Court laughed as she felt the tension between them dissipate.

"We'd better go out there," Lana said, handing her bowls full of chips and dips to carry to the living room. "I don't want to miss this."

Eric suffered through the first two rounds of the draft without his name being chosen, and Court could see by his body language he was preparing himself for disappointment. But when his name was called as the first pick in the third round, he looked like he might pass out. Everybody was cheering and patting him on the back, but after a moment he stood and ran down the hallway.

"What the hell?" Joey asked when they heard the bathroom door slam shut.

"I'll check on him," Lana said. As she walked past Court, she grabbed her wrist to stop her. When Lana looked down at her, she shook her head. "I need to see if he's okay."

"I'm sure he's fine," Court told her. Lana sat down next to her, and Court lowered her voice. "I'm pretty sure he doesn't want anyone around right now."

"Why? That makes no sense."

"He's throwing up," Court said. She nodded when Lana looked like she didn't believe her. "He's been stressed out all day. Hell, he's been stressed for weeks now. The wait's over, so his body is finally getting rid of the ball of anxiety he's been carrying around. Just give him a couple of minutes to compose himself, okay?"

"You're sure he's okay?" Lana was still skeptical, but Court could tell she knew she was probably right. Court could tell the instant Lana realized what had just happened, and she couldn't help but laugh. "Oh, my God, he was drafted! I'm going to lose my baby boy."

"I doubt you're ever going to lose him, sis," Joey said as he rested a hand on her shoulder. "He's your biggest fan."

"But he's only sixteen, and now he's going to be moving away this summer." The panic she was feeling was palpable, and Joey caught Court's attention to motion her into the kitchen.

"Don't move," Court said to Lana, and she waited for Lana to nod her agreement. She hurried after Joey. "What's up?"

"I'm going to take my parents home," he told her. "Apparently, this is hitting her and Eric harder than they'd expected, so I think it would be better for Lana if she can have her breakdown alone. Well, with you…I mean…oh hell, you know what I mean."

"Yeah, I think I do," Court said with a chuckle. "Thanks for understanding."

"I don't, really," he said with a shrug. "I thought they'd both be ecstatic."

"They are, I assure you. They just need a little time to let it all sink in."

"You'll take care of them, right?" he asked.

"I'll do what I can," she said, but wasn't entirely sure what he'd meant. Surely he knew her existence in their lives was coming to an end soon. As much as Court would love to take care of them beyond the next few weeks, she knew hoping for it was futile.

CHAPTER TWENTY-SEVEN

Can I ask something without you biting my head off?" Lana's mother said while she was helping Lana to pack up their things.

They were leaving in two days to return to Chicago, and Lana had been half expecting this conversation before now. The relationship with her parents had gotten infinitely better in the months she'd been there, and she'd be lying if she said there wasn't a part of her that wanted to stick around. Who knew how long either of them had left?

"Sure," Lana answered hesitantly.

"You seem to really like this Courtney."

"Was that a question?"

"Stop," her mother said with a chuckle. "I need to gather some information before I ask."

Lana nodded, but went on with folding her clothes and putting them in her suitcases. If she hadn't been second-guessing her decision to go home before, Court had made it especially hard the night of the draft. She'd been so sweet with both her and Eric, talking them through every fear about his future they could possibly have had. She'd even offered to visit Chicago and be her support if she needed it when he left for training camp toward the end of the summer.

She didn't want to leave. No, that wasn't entirely true. She loved living in Chicago. It was Court she didn't want to leave. The problem was, she knew she'd end up regretting it if she decided to say the hell with her life in Chicago. And if she grew to resent Court later for her own decision, it would break both their hearts. She considered asking Court to go home with her, but knew it would only create the same dilemmas for Court.

It was better this way. At least it was what she kept telling herself. Unfortunately, herself had yet to believe anything she had to say on the matter. Besides, she knew she could never expect Court to leave her home. She had another year left on her contract, and she lived right next door to her sister. It would be selfish of her to put that on Court.

"Eric likes her too," her mother said, pulling her back out of her own head.

"Yes, he does."

"Have you considered staying here and making a home with her?"

Lana stopped what she was doing and stood up straight, staring in disbelief at her mother. Where was this new acceptance coming from? It was true they'd managed to reach an understanding on Lana being a lesbian, and her mother had accepted Court being around without actually saying the words, but to actually encourage her to stay here for Court?

"Who are you, and what did you do with my mother?" she asked before she could stop herself. Her mother waved a hand at her as if to say it was no big deal as she laughed at Lana. "No, seriously, I want to know what's going on."

Lana sat on the edge of the bed and patted the mattress next to her. It took a few moments, but her mother finally sat too. She spread a T-shirt over her legs and smoothed her hands over it to try to get rid of wrinkles only she could see. Lana put a hand over hers to stop her fidgeting.

"I like her," her mother said with a shrug as though those three words explained everything. "You left without giving me and your father much of a chance to let it all sink in, and then you stayed away. It seemed easier to just pretend it wasn't real. Courtney is the first woman you've ever let us meet. We like her."

Lana laughed and threw her arms around her mother's shoulders and kissed her on the cheek. Her mother stiffened at first, not used to affection from Lana unfortunately, but she relaxed into it and Lana vowed to come visit more often. And show affection to both of her parents.

"I like her too," Lana admitted when she finally let go of her. "Probably more than I should."

"Then why are you leaving, *tesoro*?"

Lana sighed. It was the same question she'd been asking herself ever since she'd agreed to start over with Court four months earlier. She'd known then she was falling for Court. There was no way she should have continued seeing her, but there was just something about Court she couldn't resist.

"My job," Lana finally said, but her tone lacked the conviction she'd had before. She cleared her throat and nodded. "I love playing in the orchestra, Mom, and even if I signed on with another one closer to here, I'd feel like I was starting over."

"Okay, I won't push," her mother said. She went back to packing without another word.

Lana wanted to throw something, but what would that accomplish other than scaring the hell out of her mother? She took a deep breath and stood, determined to get rid of her sour mood before Eric got home from school. It was the last day of his sophomore year, and she refused to bring him down with her.

❖

Court sat on the bench in front of her locker and stared at the jersey hanging there. They'd won the league championship the night before, but she really hadn't felt like celebrating with her teammates. Lana was leaving in two days, and there wasn't anything she could do about it.

"Hey," Savannah said as she took a seat next to her.

"Hey," Court replied, forcing a smile.

"You want to talk about it?"

"What?"

"Seriously?" Savannah chuckled and shook her head. "I've known you a long time, Court. I thought we were friends. You know if you need a shoulder to cry on, I'm here for you, right?"

Court fought down the lump in her throat but didn't trust herself to speak. Instead, she just nodded. Before she'd met Lana, she was happy with her life. At least she'd thought she was. She knew now she'd only been kidding herself. And now that Lana was really leaving, she was beyond miserable. She hadn't talked to anyone about it, but she had a feeling if she talked to Savannah and not Gail, Gail would never forgive her.

"I do know that," Court said after a few moments. "And I appreciate it. I just don't think I'm ready to cry on anyone's shoulder yet."

"Okay, well, you know where to find me," Savannah said with a shrug.

Court sat there for a few minutes after Savannah walked away. She'd thought many times over the past couple of days about telling Lana again that she didn't want her to go, but she knew it was pointless. Lana had made it clear she was returning to Chicago, and Court resigned herself to having to just push it aside and move on. Unfortunately, she had a feeling moving on from Lana wasn't going to be so easy.

"Court," Gail said from the other side of the empty locker room. Most of the team had cleaned out their gear the night before. Court looked up and saw Gail motion for her to come into her office.

"What's up?" Court asked, taking a seat in front of her desk.

Gail shut the door before taking her own seat, and Court thought she looked like she had bad news. Gail opened her mouth but then shook her head and closed it again. She met Court's eyes and sighed.

"What's going on, Gail?"

"I don't know how to say this," Gail said, looking pissed off as she ran a hand through her hair. "I just got off the phone with the owner."

"We just won the championship, so I doubt they fired you," Court said, trying to lighten the mood. Gail looked sick when she tried to smile at her. "Did they sell the team?"

"They signed Jen Hilton to a multi-year contract," Gail finally said, appearing to find something fascinating on her desk. "And they're not going to exercise their option for the extra year on yours."

"So they're cutting me loose? Buying out my contract?" The thought didn't affect Court the way she'd always feared it would. She felt a strange kind of peace she didn't fully understand.

"Not exactly," Gail said. She stood and walked to the window overlooking the locker room. "You're still required to play the final year of your contract, but I think they're shopping your name around for a trade."

"You've got to be kidding me," Court said, finally feeling some of the anger she'd expected. She got to her feet and paced in the small area behind the chairs. "I have a no-trade clause."

"Well, technically, what you have is the right to refuse any trade." Gail faced her and took her hand. "Maybe it will end up being a better opportunity for you."

"Opportunity for what?" Court laughed even though there was no humor in the situation. "*We* just won the championship, and I'll be thirty-six at the end of next season. It's not like I'll be able to go to a team to have a chance to *win it all* before I retire, so what fucking opportunities do you think I'll have?"

"Just promise me you'll keep your mind open to it," Gail said. Court didn't understand where this could possibly be coming from. She tried to pull her hand out of Gail's grasp but Gail wouldn't let it go. "I don't want to see your career end because of Hilton. I'd like to see you go somewhere where they might offer you another year or two."

"Fine." Court agreed only to end the conversation, but she had no intention of accepting any trade they tried to make. She had enough on her mind at the moment.

"Thank you," Gail said with a small smile. "Not that this is any more pleasant, but when is Lana leaving?"

"Saturday morning."

"You want to come for dinner tomorrow night? Lana and Eric are invited too, of course."

"No, her brother is having a party for them at Caruso's," Court said, thinking she didn't really want to go. She didn't want to say good-bye to them. "Why don't you and Bill and the kids come? Pizza's always a popular choice for them, isn't it?"

"No, they hate pizza," Gail said, rolling her eyes. Court found herself laughing at the sarcastic tone. "Maybe we will. I'll talk to Bill about it tonight and let you know."

CHAPTER TWENTY-EIGHT

Eric wasn't having a good time. Lana looked around at the people in the restaurant. He'd invited a few of the friends he'd made at school and on the hockey team, but he was sulking alone at a table in the corner. She started to head in his direction, but a hand on her arm stopped her before she'd gotten very far.

"Let me?" Court asked.

"Sure," Lana said with a nod. She briefly covered Court's hand before she turned to go find her brother. He was in the kitchen, of course. Where else would he be? She was surprised to find their father there with him. Their mother had made him promise to consider retirement after his heart attack, and he'd agreed. Yet here he was, making pizzas like he'd never been away from it.

"Hey, sis," Joey said as he cut a pepperoni pie. "Mom doesn't know he's in here, so don't say anything to her."

"You're kidding yourself if you really think she doesn't know everything that goes on where the two of you are concerned," Lana told him before giving her father a kiss on the cheek.

"You've got that right," her father said, laughing.

"Sometimes I think the woman has eyes in the back of her head."

"Just take it easy, okay, Daddy?" she said.

"Yes, yes," he said, patting her arm and going right back to what he was doing.

"Lana, come here for a minute," Joey said, wiping his hands on his apron.

"What? You going to put me to work?"

"At your own party? What do you think I am?"

"A workaholic, and you expect everyone else to be one too."

She joined him in the back of the kitchen, far enough away from their father so he wouldn't be able to hear them.

"Why are you leaving?" Joey asked.

"What are you talking about?"

"In case you haven't noticed, your son isn't too happy about going back to Chicago, and there's a woman out there who's crazy about you." Joey stared at her, obviously waiting for a response, but she was failing in her attempt to come up with an answer he'd find believable. "And then there's the pesky little problem of you being crazy about her, too."

"You don't know anything about it, Joey," she said, feeling overly defensive. "We've talked about this. And Court and I have talked about it too. A lot. We both knew it wasn't going to be long-term."

"Yeah, you're pretty good at giving everyone your stock answer, sis, but you don't want to leave her, do you?" He crossed his arms and nodded, knowing he was right, which only made her more defensive. "Why do you have to be so stubborn all the time?"

"I take after Dad," she said, her own exasperation matching his.

"No shit," he muttered.

"Just let it go, okay? I have obligations in Chicago, and she's got a life here."

She turned to walk back to the dining area, but he grabbed her by the arm to stop her.

"What about Eric?" he asked. "Don't you care he'd rather stay here?"

"Eric will be going to Canada in a few months, so he won't care where I live."

She pulled her arm out of his grasp and stalked away. Why wouldn't everyone just let her live her own life? Things would have been so much simpler if she'd never come back here in the first place.

❖

"What are you doing over here by yourself?" Court asked when she took a seat across the table from Eric. He had a glass of soda in front of him and he kept his attention on it while she spoke. He just shook his head in response. "Tell me what's going on, buddy."

"Why can't you come to Chicago with us?" he asked.

Court realized in that moment even though Eric conducted himself as a young man, he was still emotionally immature. At the end of the day, he was still a kid. She hung her head slightly and rubbed her hands together as she considered how best to answer his question. She took a deep breath, realizing it was best to be honest with him.

"I wish I could," she said finally. "I have obligations here, Eric. I'm under contract with the Warriors."

"Then why can't we just stay here? I don't want to go back to Chicago." He finally looked at her then, and she was afraid he was going to start crying. He looked away quickly and wiped at his face. "She's happy here. With you. She isn't happy there."

What the hell was she supposed to say? She glanced around the room, not seeing Lana anywhere. Eric's friends were laughing about something at another table, and Maria Caruso was talking with Lori, who'd brought Court's niece and nephew to the party. She focused on Eric again, but waited until he looked back at her before speaking again.

"Your mom and I, we aren't…"

"Aren't what?" he asked when she faltered.

"We aren't in a permanent relationship," Court finally managed to say. She leaned back in her seat and scrubbed her face with her hand. She couldn't tell him she wanted it that way, because it didn't seem right to mention it to him without saying something to Lana about it. "We both have lives separate from each other."

"So you've been dating other women while you were seeing her?"

Court almost laughed at the look of indignation he gave her, but she knew instinctively it wouldn't be a good idea. "I'm not like that, Eric. Your mom and I, we enjoy each other's company. I like spending time with both of you." She breathed a sigh of relief when she saw Lana heading their way.

"Can I join this party, or is it private?" Lana asked. Court scooted over to give her room in the booth next to her. She sat and looked between the two of them. "Why so serious?"

Instead of answering, Eric grabbed his soda and started to leave the table. Court wanted to tell him how much she cared for him, but with Lana there, it didn't seem like the right time. She wanted him to know he could call her anytime, for anything. She felt a connection with him she didn't want to lose.

"Okay," Lana said, drawing the word out as she turned her body to face Court. "You want to tell me what that was about?"

"He doesn't understand," Court said. *And neither do I,* she wanted to add, but she bit her tongue. Trying to make Lana feel bad for doing what Court knew she'd do from the beginning wouldn't be fair to either of them.

"Understand what?"

"That you and I aren't a permanent thing." Court covered Lana's hand resting on the table and looked at her. "I tried to explain it to him, but…"

"He's worried about me," Lana said. Court looked at her without even trying to hide her confusion. Lana smiled. "He knows he's leaving in a few months, and he's worried about me being alone. I've never been alone since he was born. Well, you know, the occasional weekends he spent with his father, but not for any longer than a couple of days."

"You've never been in a relationship?"

"I've dated some, but my first priority has always been him."

Court nodded and was struck by the knowledge that with each new thing she learned about Lana, she fell a little more in love with her. She hoped to God she'd be able to survive Lana leaving in the morning.

CHAPTER TWENTY-NINE

Court's heart was pounding in her chest, and she felt like she might pass out. The pain in her chest wasn't something she'd ever experienced before, and she wasn't sure of the best way to handle it. It dawned on her this was what it felt like to have a broken heart. She glanced over at Lana, who was driving, and tried not to think about the fact this was going to be their last night together. Part of her had seriously considered just going home by herself, but there was no way she could not be with Lana to at least attempt a proper good-bye.

"You're thinking an awful lot tonight, Courtney Court," she said with a quick look in her direction. She tapped Court on the side of her head. "I think I can hear the wheels turning in there."

"Just a little sad," Court told her with a small smile. "I can't believe you're leaving in the morning."

"You aren't going to get all emotional on me, are you?"

Court forced a laugh and shook her head. "No, I won't." She turned her head to look out the passenger window and sighed. She hated feeling like this. She was in love with Lana, and she didn't feel as though she could admit it to her because she knew it wasn't what Lana wanted. Lana had made it clear from the beginning this was merely casual between them, and Court had failed in keeping her heart out of the equation. She put a hand on Lana's thigh. "I promise. No emotions."

"Good," Lana said. "Because it's going to be hard enough to say good-bye to you."

They were silent the rest of the way to Lana's house. Eric had left the party early and gotten a ride home from a friend. Lana was planning on leaving early, and he wanted to get a good night's sleep.

"Glass of wine?" Lana asked once they were inside the house.

Court nodded and hung both their jackets in the closet before following her into the kitchen. Instead of taking a seat at the table, she stepped in behind Lana and slid her arms around her waist, resting her chin on Lana's shoulder.

"I'm going to miss this, you know?" she asked before kissing her just below her ear, which caused Lana to tilt her head back. "Just sitting here and having a glass—I mean plastic cup—of wine with you at the end of the day."

"Me too." Lana sighed and turned in her arms.

Court kissed her, intent on memorizing everything about Lana, from the way her fingers played at the ends of her hair as their tongues slid together, to the way her body molded perfectly with her own. She hoped it would be something to get her through the long lonely nights to come.

"Damn, you sure know how to kiss," Lana said, breathless after pulling away.

"It's probably a good thing you're leaving," Court said, resting her forehead against Lana's. "I think if we spent much more time together, I might start to really like you."

Lana laughed, but Court thought it sounded forced. She

took a step back and picked up the plastic cups of wine Lana had poured. After handing one to Lana, she touched the cups together. "To the most incredible woman I've ever had the pleasure of knowing."

Lana smiled, touched by the sentiment and surprised Court had spoken the words she was thinking. She took a sip before taking Court's cup and placing them both back on the counter. She touched Court's cheek and watched the storm of emotions swirling through her beautiful blue eyes.

"Come to bed with me," she said, and Court nodded. Lana tried not to think about how lost she was going to be without Court. Hell, she missed her already, and she wasn't even gone yet. If she considered how much it was going to rock her in the morning, she might just crumble right there on the threshold of her bedroom.

"What's wrong?" Court asked, pulling Lana out of her own head.

Lana blinked as she realized she was standing just outside the door and staring at her bed. She plastered on a smile and looked at Court. She didn't want Court to see the sadness in her eyes.

"Nothing's wrong," she lied with a shake of her head. She turned to fully face Court and began to undress her. "I was just thinking about how much I want you."

Once they were both fully naked, Lana led her to the bed and pushed her onto her back before crawling up her body and straddling her hips. She leaned over and held herself up with her hands on the mattress on either side of Court's head.

"I don't want this night to end," Court said, her voice barely above a whisper as they stared into each other's eyes.

Lana felt as though Court was seeing into her soul. For all the time they spent having sex, this was the only time Lana experienced this depth of intimacy. It made her uncomfortable. As she closed her eyes to keep Court from seeing what she was feeling, Court touched her cheek.

"Can I just hold you?" she asked, causing Lana to open her eyes again. Lana was sure she looked as surprised as she felt, but she nodded. "It's not that I don't want to do this, but I really just want to hold you in my arms right now. We have all night, right?"

"Yes," Lana said as she rolled off and allowed Court to pull her close. She stayed there with her head on Court's chest, Court's arms around her, and the strong steady heartbeat sounding in her ear. She finally relaxed when Court's breathing evened out, indicating she'd fallen asleep, and she sighed. The quiet rhythm of Court's breathing and heartbeat finally lulled Lana to sleep after what seemed like an eternity.

❖

Lana watched as Eric and Court shoved the last of their things into her car, and then Eric walked back into the house, his head down as he went past her. She tried to stop him with a hand on his arm, but he pulled away from her and continued on. She shook her head and saw Court watching her with a sad smile.

"So," Court said, glancing at the house. "That was the last of it?"

"Yes. I want to thank you for all your help," Lana told her. She'd always hated saying good-bye. Especially now, with Court. It was only six in the morning, but Lana had promised her parents she and Eric would stop to have breakfast before heading out.

"No need to thank me," Court said with a shrug. She

looked down at her feet and shoved her hands into her back pockets. When she met Lana's eyes again, she noticed Court's eyes were filled with unshed tears. "Can I call you?"

Even though Lana knew a clean break would be for the best, she nodded. She was afraid losing all contact with Court would rip her heart out.

"You'd better." Lana smiled and went to hug Court. "Don't get into any more fights with Jen Hilton."

"I won't." Court chuckled as she buried her face in Lana's hair. "Unless she starts it."

Lana pulled away and decided she couldn't delay this good-bye any longer. She sighed and shook her head. "I guess that's as good as I can hope for. I should really get going."

"Yeah, right," Court said, nodding. "Can I go say good-bye to Eric?"

"Of course." Lana followed her into the house to find him. He was sitting on the couch staring at the wall and looking more sullen than Lana had ever seen him. "Eric, come say good-bye."

He didn't move, not even to glance in their direction. She started to walk closer to him, but Court stopped her.

"It's okay," she said quietly.

Lana watched as she went to sit next to Eric. He looked at Court, and Lana saw he too had unshed tears. Court hugged him and then stood again, but said something to him Lana couldn't hear. He nodded before resuming his staring contest with the wall.

"Good-bye, Lana," Court said before kissing her gently on the mouth. "Drive safe."

"Thanks," she said, and then Court was gone. For a moment, she felt as though she'd fall apart. It was hard to breathe, and she wanted nothing more than to run out the door after her, but she heard the car start and then pull out of the driveway. She took a moment to steady herself before joining Eric. "Come on, it's time to go."

"I don't want to go."

"Eric," she said, tired of fighting this battle he'd been intent on waging for the past week.

"Why can't we just stay here?"

"I remember very distinctly last October when you didn't want to come here, and now you want to stay?"

"I like it here." He shrugged, but refused to look at her. "There's family here. There's nobody back in Chicago."

"What about your friends? The school you didn't want to leave? What about Sandy?" Lana wasn't above manipulation, and she knew the mention of the girl he had a crush on back home would get his attention.

"So I get to see her for a couple of months and then I'll be gone to training camp." He finally looked at her and she knew he realized what she was doing.

"Exactly," she said. "You'll be gone. So why does it matter to you where I am after you go to training camp?"

"Damn it, Mom," he said. She didn't like it when he swore, but she'd learned to pick her battles over the years. She knew he only said it in the heat of the moment, so she let it slide. She wasn't naïve enough to think he didn't swear around his friends, but he rarely did it in front of her. "I don't want you to be alone."

"I know you don't," she said, reaching over to take his hand. "And I love that you have this protective streak, but, Eric, I'm almost thirty-seven years old. I'm pretty sure I can take care of myself. And what makes you think I won't be happy to finally be able to have some time alone after the past sixteen years of having you underfoot?"

He laughed at that, and she smiled. It was the first genuine smile she'd had in days, and it felt good. She finally managed to talk him into leaving, so they headed to breakfast with the family. She wasn't looking forward to saying good-bye to them either. She was just happy the relationship with her parents had improved so much.

CHAPTER THIRTY

Lana smiled at Eric as he was getting ready to leave for his girlfriend's house. It was the Fourth of July and she was realizing, not for the first time, exactly how much she was missing Court. How was it she could have woven her way into Lana's life so completely in just a few months? Especially when Lana had been so determined not to let it happen. She shook her head.

"Are you okay, Mom?" Eric asked. He sat next to her on the couch and put his arm around her as he spoke. "I don't have to go, you know."

"I'm fine," she assured him, patting him on the knee. "Go enjoy dinner with your girlfriend and her family, and enjoy the fireworks. Just make sure you're home by midnight."

"I'll be home before midnight." He started to get up, but apparently changed his mind. "You're thinking about her, aren't you?"

"Who?" Lana looked at him and knew immediately she wasn't going to fool him. She sighed and gave him a small smile. "Yeah, I am."

"I can always tell, you know."

"How?"

"You have a certain look, like you're sad, but not a normal kind of sad, you know what I mean?" he asked, looking like he was having trouble coming up with the right words to adequately describe it.

"No, I don't."

"When you get this look, it's like I know I can't do anything to cheer you up." He thought for a moment, then glanced at her again. "Like you're melancholy. Is that the right word?"

"Maybe, but it sounds a little depressing." She smiled to show him she was joking, but she had to admit he was pretty right on with his assessment.

"I miss her."

"I do too, Eric," she said. "More than I thought I would."

"Are you ever going to tell her how you feel?"

"What are you talking about?"

"Come on, Mom," he said, exasperated. "You love her, right?"

There was no reason to lie to him. Aside from the fact she never lied to him anyway, he was obviously more intuitive and intelligent than he had any right to be at sixteen. Lying just seemed as if it would be insulting to him. She finally nodded.

"You need to tell her."

"Maybe. Someday. I don't know."

"Are adults always so wishy-washy?" He laughed when she gave him a look of shock. "If so, I don't want to grow up."

"Get out of here," she told him as she shoved him away. "If you have a girlfriend, then I'd say you're already well on your way to growing up."

"Are you sure you won't come with me?" he asked as he got to his feet. "They said there'd be plenty of food."

"I'll be fine, Eric," she said, walking him to the door. "Have fun."

He kissed her on the cheek, and then he was gone. She leaned against the door and sighed as she reflected on the things he'd said. She did love Court, didn't she? It wasn't a new revelation, but she hadn't allowed herself the luxury of thinking about it too much. If she did, it would only make her...melancholy. She laughed and went to the kitchen to figure out what she wanted to eat for dinner.

She'd never admit it to Eric, but she actually looked forward to nights like this. Time alone wasn't a commodity she'd had much of since he'd been born. But then it hit her that in just over a month, he was going to be leaving for Quebec and what would be the beginning of his hockey career. She'd have more time alone than she'd know what to do with then. The thought didn't make her happy.

She heated a can of soup and settled in to watch a movie. She found herself wondering what Court was doing, and considered calling her. They talked on the phone once in a while, and sometimes even made video calls, but she figured she was probably busy tonight with her sister, or maybe Gail and Bill.

After all, most people spent holidays with family and friends, and although Lana had been invited to watch the fireworks with her own friends, she'd opted to stay home. She was beginning to regret the decision now because she was having a difficult time thinking about anything other than Court.

She picked her phone up again and scrolled to Court's name, hesitating for a moment before tapping the call button. She could always leave a message if she didn't answer, right? Just to say hello. She didn't have to tell her she was missing her.

"Hey, Lana," Court said, breaking into Lana's thoughts.

"Courtney Court, hey," she said, sitting up straighter. She

was startled she'd answered the phone and was caught off guard.

"You sound surprised." Court chuckled. "You did call me, right?"

"I did, yes. I didn't expect to get you, though." Lana was struggling to find something to say. "I thought you'd be enjoying the fireworks with your sister. I was just going to leave a message."

"Well, now you don't have to." Court smiled and waved a hand at Lori, who was motioning for her to hurry up. They could see the fireworks from her backyard, and the kids were excited they were about to start. "And we are about to watch the fireworks."

"I won't keep you then," Lana said, sounding like her cheerfulness was forced. "I just wanted to say hello."

"Tell Eric I said hi." Court made her way to the back deck as she talked. She didn't want to hang up. They didn't talk nearly as often as she'd like, but on the other hand, the more they talked, the more she wished Lana was here with her. "Can I call you in a few days?"

"Sure, yeah," Lana said. "I'm sorry I interrupted your evening."

"Lana, you could never interrupt anything," Court told her. She took a seat next to Lori and sighed. "I love hearing from you. I'll talk to you soon, okay?"

"You didn't have to hang up," Lori said when Court set the phone on the small table between them. "I know you like talking to her."

"I can call her anytime," Court said with a smile. "I only get to spend the Fourth of July with Ryan and Alice once a year."

"Aren't you sweet?" Lori rolled her eyes and Court

laughed. They watched the beginning of the show as the kids squealed in delight. "You haven't told her yet, have you?"

"Told her what?"

"That you love her. God, you can be dense sometimes."

"I don't," Court said, wondering if God would strike her down for lying to her sister.

"Bullshit." Lori didn't look at her. "You can kid yourself all you want, but it's true."

"Maybe she and I can explore our possibilities when my hockey days are over." It was as close as Court would get to admitting her feelings. Maybe as long as the word stayed in her head and never passed her lips, it wouldn't be true.

"Whatever," Lori said. "You're going to grow old all alone."

"Maybe I will, but if I do, it will be my choice," Court said, stretching her legs out in front of her. She'd never thought much about growing old, but the thought of doing it alone made her uneasy. She closed her eyes and allowed her mind to wander. She'd never met anyone she wanted to build a future with. Until Lana. Just thinking about her brought a smile to her lips and caused a fluttering in her chest.

Yes, she did love Lana. As she opened her eyes again, she made a promise to herself. If she ever actually saw Lana again, she would tell her how she felt. It just didn't seem right to her to make that kind of declaration over the telephone. If Lana didn't feel the same way about her, at least she wouldn't spend the rest of her life wondering if she'd blown her chance at true happiness.

CHAPTER THIRTY-ONE

Court spent the next few weeks before the start of training camp trying her damnedest to bury herself in work. She'd done the commercial for Caruso's and had enjoyed the time she spent as a result with Lana's family. Plus she'd sold more houses in the few months since Lana had left than she had in the two years prior to meeting her, which was not only good for her personal bank account but was also good for Gail and Bill, since they owned the realty company.

She kept up with Lana over the phone and on video chat only sporadically, mostly because Court hated the feeling of loss she experienced every time they hung up. They never talked about anything too serious. Mostly they talked about Eric, who had just left for Quebec and his first ever training camp. Court was really pulling for him to make the team even though it would be tough for a sixteen-year-old his first time out. It was more likely he wouldn't get a spot on the team until the following year. Court had offered to go with them when Lana took him to Canada, but Lana insisted she'd be fine doing it by herself.

Court was relieved with every day that passed she hadn't been traded. At least not yet. She knew from Gail the team was trying hard to work out a deal with a team she might be willing to go to, and her teammates weren't happy about any of it. Except for Hilton. If it meant Court would be off the team, she was all for it and made no apologies. Court couldn't deny she'd be happier playing on a team against Hilton. At least then she could fight her without worrying about ruining the team unity.

The first day of training camp started out fine. Probably because Hilton was late getting on the ice with the rest of the team. Court was by the bench talking to Gail when Hilton skated over to them.

"I hear you're getting traded, Abbott," she said, her smile ear to ear. Gail rolled her eyes at Court, who just shook her head. "I told you I was the future here. You might as well pack your shit and get out of town."

"You know what I love about you, Hilton?" Court asked, almost laughing at the look of disgust she now wore. "Absolutely nothing. It might actually be worth it to get traded to a team within the division so I can catch you with your head down at center ice."

"Is that a threat?" Hilton asked as she shot a look at Gail. Court shook her head again and started to skate away. "Are you threatening me, Abbott?"

"Grow up," Court said over her shoulder. She half expected Hilton to come after her, but she didn't stop or even look back until she'd reached Savannah and Kelly behind the far goal.

"What's she yapping about?" Kelly asked, tilting her head toward Hilton.

Court glanced over her shoulder and saw Gail yelling at Hilton. She couldn't hear anything being said, but she could tell by the red in Gail's face she was pissed. Court chuckled and turned her attention back to her line mates.

"Just being her humble self," Court said.

"That'll be the day." Savannah rolled her eyes as she spoke. "Please tell us you're going to reject any trade they try to make. I don't think I can suffer through a season of her without you here as a buffer."

"I'm the one she has a problem with," Court said. They skated to center ice when Gail blew her whistle to start the practice. "If I'm not here, she probably won't be so antagonistic."

"You know we don't want you to go, right?" Kelly asked. Court looked at her and smiled as she nodded. Court didn't want to leave either. In fact, she was planning on staying right where she was. She really couldn't imagine playing anywhere else.

Gail split them into two teams so she could get a feel for how the newcomers would fit in with the veterans. Court was on one team and Hilton on the other, causing Court to wonder what the hell Gail was thinking. If Hilton was willing to trip Court when they were on the same team—in an actual game, no less—then what might she do if they were on opposite sides during a practice game?

"No hits! I want to see you play, not knock the shit out of each other!" Gail said. A few of the women groaned but some actually looked relieved. Court honestly didn't care one way or the other. She knew Gail didn't want anyone getting hurt, but if someone couldn't handle a hard hit in the corner, wouldn't it be better to know from the outset?

Of course she put Hilton and Court against each other for the first faceoff. Was Gail trying to start something between the two of them? Court glared at Gail for a moment before readying herself for the puck to drop. She was going to have to have a chat with Gail when this was over.

When the puck dropped, Hilton ignored it and went right

for Court. She brought her stick up and caught Court under the chin, which caused her to fall backward onto the ice. Hilton came down on top of her and started punching her in the head. She was immediately pulled off her and Savannah knelt down next to Court.

"Are you all right?" she asked Court, helping her to get to her feet. "You're bleeding."

"Of course I am," Court said after removing her gloves and touching her chin. She caught Hilton's eye and tried to pull away from Savannah to go after her, but Savannah held tight to her arm. "Just give me one shot at her."

"I'd love to, but Gail would probably bench us all, and then none of us would be on the team anymore." Savannah pulled her to the bench and found a towel for her to staunch the bleeding. "You're probably going to need stitches."

"Let me see it," Gail said as she joined them. She reached between them and pulled the towel away for a moment. "Get in the locker room and have it taken care of."

"Are you going to do anything about this shit?" Court asked when Gail started to skate away. Savannah obviously didn't want anything to do with this, and she took the opportunity to make her escape.

"What the hell do you want me to do, Court? I've benched her, I've fined her, I've begged the front office to do something about it," Gail said, her frustration with the situation coming through. "What do you suggest I do?"

They stared at each other, neither of them willing to back down. Court decided she really hated Hilton. She was a constant thorn in her side since the day they'd met almost a year ago, and now she was the cause of friction between Court and her best friend. Court finally shook her head and looked away.

"Court, I'm sorry," Gail said, looking as pissed off as

Court felt. "I really am. I don't think any of us have had to deal with someone quite like her before. I'm flying by the seat of my pants here. Maybe I should just let you beat the crap out of her. That would teach her a lesson."

They shared a laugh over something they both knew Gail would never do. Court sighed and pulled the towel away to see she was still bleeding. God, she hated having to get stitched up. She shrugged and looked at Gail again.

"I would seriously love to put her in her place," she said. She glanced across the ice and saw Hilton holding court with a bunch of the newbies at camp this year. No doubt they looked up to her. Court felt her heart sink just a little as the reality of her professional situation hit her. Her eyes wandered around the arena before finally settling on Gail again. "Any word on a trade yet?"

"No," Gail answered, looking sad. "I'll let you know when I hear anything."

"I hate for this to be causing problems for us, Gail." Court picked up the gloves she'd dropped on the ice. "I love you, you know that, right?"

"Yeah, and I love you, too. A spoiled little brat isn't going to change what we have."

Court headed for the locker room as Gail turned and skated back to the rest of the team. As much as she would love to close out her career here, the writing was on the wall. If she refused a trade, this is what her life would be like for the entirety of the season. Court wasn't sure she had the energy to deal with the chaos for the next eight months.

❖

Court was stitched up and getting ready to head back out to the ice when Hilton came into the locker room. Alone. *Fuck.*

Obviously, she only came in to grab a new stick because she went right to where they were leaning against the wall outside the office. She saw Court sitting in front of her locker, and apparently just couldn't help herself.

"Why haven't you been traded yet?" she asked. Court slammed her locker shut and got to her feet to face her. Hilton moved toward her, stopping close enough so Court could feel her breath on her cheek. "I can't wait for you to be gone."

"You know, for someone who has such a problem with me being a lesbian, you certainly have no qualms about getting into my personal space." Court didn't move, not even when Hilton laughed in her face. "You know what they say about people who are the most vocal about their hatred toward anyone in the LGBTQ community."

"Are you trying to insinuate I'm gay?" The laughter was gone as quickly as it came, and there was a fire in her eyes. "You people won't be happy until everyone is gay, will you?"

"*You people?*" Court laughed now, mostly because of the absurdity of her comment. Unfortunately, it appeared to infuriate Hilton even more. She took another step toward Court, even though there hadn't seemed to be enough room between them to begin with, and Court refused to back down. "I don't give a shit who you, or anyone else, sleep with. And I'd appreciate it if you'd keep *your* mind out of *my* bedroom."

Court tried to muscle her way past, but Hilton stepped with her. Tried to trip her, actually, and something in Court snapped. She took Hilton's jersey in her fist and slammed her against the locker. She took no joy in the fear she saw on Hilton's face, but it didn't stop her either. She stood so her nose was less than an inch from Hilton's as she spoke.

"Stay the fuck away from me, do you understand?" she asked, her voice low just in case anyone else walked in. Hilton nodded and swallowed hard. Court twisted the jersey and raised her so Hilton's feet weren't touching the ground. "Mess with me again, or anyone else on this team, and I won't walk away from you. I'm sure you're smart enough to grasp what I'm saying."

Court released her after another good push into the locker, and Hilton fell to the floor. Court grabbed her gear and headed back out to the ice without another word. By the look of panic in Hilton's eye, Court knew she wouldn't have another problem with her. She was nothing but a bully, and Court's father had taught her the only way to stop a bully was to stand up to them.

Chapter Thirty-two

Three games into the season, Gail showed up on Court's doorstep just as she was sitting down to dinner with Lori, Ryan, and Alice. Court could tell there was something going on, and even before Gail said a word, Court knew why she was there.

"Come in," Court said as she stepped aside. When Gail saw Lori and the kids, she stopped and turned back to Court.

"I didn't realize you were in the middle of dinner," she said. "I can come back later."

"No, you're here now, and I'm pretty sure what you have to say is going to have an impact on Lori too," Court said, shaking her head. She took her seat at the kitchen table and Lori pulled Alice into her lap so Gail could sit as well.

"Caruso's?" Gail asked, eying the pizza in the middle of the table.

"They do have good food, and it doesn't hurt they offered me free pizza whenever I want it for doing their commercial," Court said. She picked up a slice and placed it on a paper plate she then handed to Gail. When Gail opted to take a bite before telling them why she was there, Court crossed her arms over her chest and leaned against the back of her chair. "Just tell me who I've been traded to so I can pretend to think about it before saying no."

Gail took her time setting her slice down and wiping her hands. She looked at Lori, who Court was sure was just as anxious as she was to find out. When she finally met Court's eyes, she sighed.

"The Wolves," she said, and Court's mind raced along with her pulse. "They want you to report tomorrow. I booked you a flight for the afternoon and will be taking you to the airport."

"Where are the Wolves?" Lori asked.

"Chicago," Court said, her voice quieter than she'd expected. Gail held her gaze and gave her a small smile as she nodded. Court's first thought was to call Lana and tell her, but then before she could even form another thought, she worried if Lana might not think this was a good thing. "Really? Chicago?"

"Yeah," Gail said, looking a little worried. "I thought you might be happy about it."

"I might be if I didn't have this gnawing feeling you orchestrated the whole thing," Court said, the fog finally beginning to dissipate.

Gail shook her head and held her hands up. "They were trying to trade you. I swear I had nothing to do with that part of it. However, I did tell them I thought the only place you would even consider would be Chicago. Was I wrong?"

"No, you weren't," Court said. "But what if she doesn't want me there? Or did you involve her in this too?"

"I haven't talked to her since the night we won the championship, Court, I promise. I didn't even know they were going to seek a trade for you until the next day."

"Why wouldn't she want you there?" Lori asked, sounding confused. "I thought the only reason things ended was because your permanent homes were so far apart. You're in love with her whether you want to admit it or not, and unless I've completely lost my ability to read people, she feels the same about you. There's no question Eric fell head over heels for you."

"Or maybe us living so far apart was just a convenient excuse to end it. Maybe she never had any intention of taking things beyond this past spring, and it was a way of keeping her distance." Court didn't want to believe the things she was suggesting, but it had seemed to her Lana leaving wasn't nearly as hard for Lana as it had been for her.

"You can't seriously think that, can you?" Gail asked, sounding completely shocked. She looked at Lori. "I agree with your assessment. There's no way they aren't both in love."

"I know, right?" Lori nodded as she tried to help Alice get another slice of pizza. Court chuckled when mother and child both ended up wearing more of the pizza than Alice was actually getting into her mouth. "I honestly think the two of them were the only ones who couldn't see it."

"Bill said the same thing." Gail laughed along with Lori, but Court didn't find the humor in any of this.

"I am sitting right here, you know," she said, her eyes darting back and forth between them.

"Call her," Lori finally said to her. "You'll see I'm right, Court. I know she'll be happy about it."

"I haven't said yes to the trade yet, in case you've both failed to notice." Court glared at them both, hoping they couldn't see how excited she was at the prospect of living so close to Lana. She got up and went to the sink, her back to the table.

"You aren't seriously thinking about saying no, are you?" Gail asked. "There was an offer from Pittsburgh they really wanted to pull the trigger on, but I stepped in to do you a favor.

If you don't accept the trade, you're going to make me look like an idiot."

"Well, we can't have that, can we?" Court grinned as she turned to face them again. Gail jumped up and ran to hug her, and Court laughed. "But I'll never forgive you if she doesn't want to pick up where we left off."

❖

Court had tried to call Lana later the same evening, but she wasn't able to get in touch with her. She left a generic message, just saying she'd try her again tomorrow and there was no need for her to call her back. Of course, the fact Lana *didn't* call her back caused a bit of anxiety, but Court held out hope she could see her face-to-face before Lana learned of the trade on her own. It hadn't taken much to convince Joey to give her Lana's address, and she made him promise not to tell her she was coming to Chicago until she had a chance to do it herself.

She'd met with the Wolves' owners and coaching staff as soon as she got to the arena after her plane landed. They had a day off the following day, so she was told where to go for a physical then. As long as nothing unexpected came up during the exam, she was to report the day after that for her first practice with her new team.

Once she was done with her meeting, she hailed a cab and had it take her to the address Joey had given her. After a short internal debate on whether or not to get a hotel room first, she decided she could get a room later. She needed to see Lana first.

Her phone vibrated in her pocket as they drove through the city, and she pulled it out, expecting to see either Gail or Lori's name since she hadn't called either of them yet to let them know she'd arrived safely. She smiled when she saw it was Lana calling. She didn't even hesitate before answering it.

"Hey," she said.

"I am so sorry I didn't call you back sooner, but I lost my phone yesterday morning. I just now found it in the couch cushions." Lana sounded genuinely upset, and Court couldn't help but chuckle.

"No worries," she said. She really didn't want to tell her she was in the city until she got to her building, so she leaned forward. "Hold on a second, okay?"

"Sure," Lana answered. Court pulled the phone away from her ear and held it to her chest.

"How long until we get there?" she asked the driver. He told her, and she leaned back again. "Lana, can I call you back in about fifteen minutes? I'm in the middle of something."

"Yeah, of course. I'll talk to you in a few."

CHAPTER THIRTY-THREE

Lana ran her hand through her hair. She couldn't believe she'd lost her phone in the couch. And she'd panicked when she saw she'd missed a call from Court the night before. She'd gotten to where she looked forward to their phone conversations, and she was mad at herself for having missed the opportunity to talk to her. She sat on the couch now, the phone in her hand, waiting for Court to call her back.

Eric had flown home the night before, and they'd gone out for dinner. He'd been bummed to find out he'd been cut the last day of training camp, but they promised him he'd be their first call-up if a position opened on the team. He was strangely optimistic about it, which made Lana proud. He'd gone out with some of his friends that afternoon, and she knew he'd be home soon, so she really should be making dinner, but she didn't want anything to interrupt her time talking to Court.

When the phone finally rang, Lana jumped and almost dropped it on the floor. She fumbled with it to answer the call, and she felt out of breath when she finally did.

"Courtney Court," she said as she felt a smile tugging at the corners of her mouth. She felt herself relax at the first words out of Court's mouth, directly in her ear.

"Can I just say I miss you?" Court asked.

"I miss you, too," Lana said, staring at the ceiling and imagining Court there with her. So many times when they'd talked over the past few months she'd wanted to admit her feelings to Court, but felt it wouldn't be fair to her. Maybe at the end of the season if she didn't re-sign with the Warriors, she'd take a chance and tell her she loved her. A vision of Court naked flashed in her mind, and she chuckled as she shook her head.

"What's so funny?" Court asked, sounding amused.

"What are you wearing?" Lana asked instead of answering her question. She heard Court gasp on the other end of the line.

"Really? You want to do this now?" Court asked.

"Why not?"

"Um, because I'm standing outside right now," Court laughed and then let out a soft moan. "And if this is headed where I think it might be, it could be a little embarrassing."

"Not for me."

"Oh, you're bad, Ms. Caruso."

"And you like it, don't you?" Lana asked, lowering her voice. She wished Eric wasn't going to be home any minute. She'd never had phone sex before, but Court's voice was so freaking sexy right now.

There was a knock at the door, and Lana jumped to her feet as though she were about to be caught doing something she shouldn't have been doing.

"Shit," she said.

"Something wrong?" Court sounded amused again, but Lana definitely wasn't.

"Someone's at the door." Lana headed toward it but stopped, listening. Something wasn't right. She could have sworn she heard knocking from Court's end of the line at the same time. "Where are you?"

"Outside," Court answered. "I'll hold on while you answer the door. I'm not going anywhere."

"Outside where?" Lana asked, pausing with her hand on the doorknob. Her heart was racing. If she opened the door and Court wasn't there, she wasn't sure what she'd do.

"Oh, my God, Lana, you don't make trying to surprise you easy, do you?" Court laughed, and Lana heard it on the other side of the door. She pulled it open just as Court started to speak again. "Just answer the damn door."

Lana stared at her standing there, not quite believing what she was seeing. Court disconnected their call, but Lana still had her phone to her ear.

"What are you doing here?" she asked.

"I came for a visit," she answered with a sheepish grin and a shrug. "I can go if you don't want to see me though."

"Get in here," Lana said, grabbing her hand and pulling her inside the apartment. She finally shoved the phone in her pocket and threw her arms around Court's neck as she pushed the door closed with her foot. "I can't believe you're here."

"Neither can I, if I'm being honest," Court said. She pulled Lana tight against her body and kissed her. "But I have my things outside your door."

Lana released her and they brought her bags inside. Lana grabbed her hand again as soon as they were done and dragged her to the couch where they fell onto it, Lana in Court's lap kissing her again. Court slid her hands up Lana's sides under her shirt, and Lana surged against her with a whimper as she broke their kiss.

"I can't believe you're here," she said again, touching Court's face. Court chuckled and leaned her head back so it rested against the cushion.

"I can't stay," Court said, not wanting her to think she was here expecting to jump right into her bed. She hoped for it, of course, but she didn't expect it. "I need to get a hotel room before it gets too late."

"You aren't going anywhere, Courtney Court." Lana shook her head and placed a finger against Court's lips. "You're staying here with me. How long are you going to be in town?"

"Well, that depends," Court said, tightening her hold around Lana's waist.

"On what?"

"On whether or not the Wolves make the playoffs."

Lana looked at her, obviously confused. Court watched as Lana opened her mouth then closed it again, trying to figure out what the heck she was talking about. Court smiled and kissed the end of her nose as she saw the different emotions storm through Lana's beautiful brown eyes, and she nodded when it was clear Lana had figured it out.

"You've been traded?" Lana asked, her voice little more than a whisper.

"I have. I'll go for a physical tomorrow, and as long as they don't find anything wrong with me, then the trade will be finalized."

"Oh, my God, wait until Eric finds out!" Lana kissed her hard.

"I'm kind of more interested in your reaction," Court said and Lana threw her head back and laughed.

"I'm so happy I want to rip your clothes off right this minute."

"You wouldn't hear any complaints from me." Court tried to unbutton Lana's shirt, but Lana grabbed her hands before she could get even one undone.

"You'd probably complain when Eric walks in and sees you here in the living room naked."

"I thought he was in Canada." Lana got off her lap and sat next to her. Court put an arm around her and Lana immediately laid her head on her shoulder. "What happened?"

"He was cut on the last day. He got home last night."

"The last day?" Court shook her head. "I know it has to suck, but it's encouraging he stuck around that long. It means he was this close to making the team."

"That's what they told him, but as I'm sure you know, it didn't make it any easier for him to swallow." Lana laced her fingers with Court's and held her hand in her lap. "But he's actually being really mature about it. He's counting on joining the team at some point if another player gets hurt."

"I'm sure he will."

Court was surprised Lana didn't even try to pull away from her when they heard a key in the door. When they heard other voices along with Eric's though, Lana sat up and let go of her hand.

"Mom, guess what I found out?" Eric said, sounding excited. When he saw Court on the couch with her, some of the excitement drained from his face. "Oh. I guess you already know."

"Holy crap, it's really Courtney Abbott," one of the kids with Eric said.

"I told you I knew her," Eric said with a smirk. Court stood, and Eric was hugging her before she even knew what was happening. "I can't believe you're here."

"The sentiment seems to run in your family," Court said with a glance at Lana, now standing next to her. "I'm sorry I ruined your plan to tell her about the trade. If you'd gotten here a few minutes earlier, you'd have beaten me."

"It's okay," he said before walking over to his friends again. "I'm just glad you're here."

Court watched as the three kids, one girl and two boys,

pulled money out of their pockets and handed it over to Eric. The grin on his face made Court laugh out loud.

"Eric, what's going on?" Lana asked.

"They bet me I didn't know her," he said with a shrug. "How could I pass up a sure thing?"

"He has a point," Court said. She winced when Lana elbowed her in the ribs. She rubbed her side and looked at Lana with her eyes narrowed. "You could play hockey with a move like that."

"I have enough hockey players in my life, thank you," Lana said, grabbing her hand and lifting it to her lips.

"No way," said the girl as she stared at them. "Your mom is dating her? This is so freaking awesome!"

Eric threw his arm around the girl and kissed her cheek before looking at Court again. "Court, this is Sandy. My girlfriend."

"Girlfriend?" Court asked, thinking the blush on Eric's face was adorable. "Well, Sandy, it's a pleasure to meet you."

Chapter Thirty-four

They ordered takeout and spent the evening with Eric and his friends, who Court was sure would have a great time telling their other friends all about it. Everyone finally left around nine, and it was just the three of them there in the living room. Eric muted the TV and turned to face the two of them.

"So, are you living with us now?" he asked.

Court was taken off guard. She looked at Lana, who seemed to be avoiding making eye contact with her. She shook her head.

"I don't know where I'm going to live," Court answered truthfully. "I guess finding a place will have to be my first priority."

"You're welcome to stay here until you find a place," Lana said, still keeping her eyes averted.

"I think you should just move in here," Eric said. He obviously anticipated objection, because he held up a hand. "Hear me out. I'm going to be gone, hopefully sooner rather than later. No offense, Mom. I would feel better knowing you wouldn't be here alone while I'm away."

"So this is coming from your concern about me," Lana said. "You think I can't take care of myself?"

"No, that's not it," he said, looking frustrated. He looked at Court, and even though she could tell he was asking for her help here, she shook her head. He was on his own with this. "I really want you two to be together, and if it means packaging it into my concern for you being alone, I'm not above that kind of manipulation."

"Is that so?" Lana chuckled and shook her head, but she finally looked at Court. "See what I meant when I said he was fifteen going on thirty? Now I think he's sixteen going on forty. What do you think about what he's saying?"

"It's not what I was expecting when I came here," Court said, stalling to come up with a diplomatic way of responding. "I'm perfectly fine with finding my own place."

"Okay." Lana seemed to be disappointed with her response, but Court wondered if it was nothing more than wishful thinking on her part. Lana focused on Eric again. "We know your opinion, so I think it's something Court and I will need to think about and discuss in private."

Eric nodded as he looked back and forth between the two of them. After a moment, he stood and handed the remote to Lana.

"I'm going to go to bed," he said. He looked at Court. "You'll be here in the morning, right?"

"Yeah, I will," she replied. She watched him as he went to his room, and Lana snuggled closer to her as soon as he was gone.

They sat there for a while longer, but Court wasn't paying attention to what was on the TV. She wanted to know what Lana was thinking, although she wasn't sure how to bring it up. Lana shut off the TV and stood, holding a hand out to Court.

They were both silent as Lana led her into her bedroom, and she closed the door behind them before turning to face

Court, her arms sliding around her neck. Court placed her hands on Lana's hips and couldn't help it when her breath quickened. She'd been thinking about this since the moment she'd arrived and Lana had made it apparent she was happy to see her.

"I need you to touch me, Court."

Court made quick work of removing Lana's clothes. She walked her backward toward the bed, and when Lana's knees hit the edge of the mattress, she sat, but held Court's hands away from her.

"You." Lana's eyes slowly moved up Court's body, and Court felt it as though it were a physical touch. "Naked. Now."

Court removed her own T-shirt and bra while Lana worked on unbuttoning her pants and pushing them down her legs. She stepped out of her jeans and stood naked before Lana.

"Damn, you have an incredible body," Lana said. She moved quickly so she was under the covers, then held them up for Court to join her. Court crawled in and straddled her legs, her mouth closing over Lana's nipple as Lana pulled the covers up so they were over Court's head. "I've missed you so much, Courtney Court."

Court pulled her mouth away from Lana's breast and slid off her to stretch out next to her. Lana turned her head and touched Court's cheek, searching her eyes with obvious concern.

"What's wrong?" she asked, and Court shook her head.

"Nothing is wrong. In fact, everything feels so right to me for the first time in what feels like forever." Court let her fingers trace the lines of Lana's face as she spoke. "I wanted to beg you not to come back to Chicago, but I didn't think it was right to ask you to give up your life here. I wanted to tell you I was falling in love with you, but I knew it wasn't what you wanted."

Lana's breath hitched as the meaning of Court's words washed over her. She pressed her lips to Court's because she couldn't *not* kiss her in that moment. She pulled Court on top of her as she let her legs fall open to allow her room to settle in.

"Tell me again," Lana said, her heart racing and her head swimming from the ecstasy of hearing Court expressing what she herself was feeling.

"What?"

"You know what," Lana said, smiling. "Tell me again."

"I'm in love with you, Lana Caruso," she said breathlessly.

"I'm in love with you too," she said as she wrapped her legs around Court's thighs and pressed into her. "Even if it wasn't what I thought I wanted. I know now that I don't want to know what it's like to not love you."

"What are you saying?" Court thrust her hips slowly into her, and Lana closed her eyes as she tilted her head back.

"I want you to move in here," Lana said, quickly losing her ability to think as Court drove her closer to the edge. She put her hands on Court's hips and held tight, trying to make her stop moving. "Stop. Just for a second. I can't think when you're doing that."

"Doing what?" Court asked with a knowing grin. She yelped when Lana pinched her ass and then slapped her. Lana cupped Court's face between her hands and gazed into her eyes.

"Do you want to live with me?"

"Yes," Court said. "You really need to ask?"

"I just wanted to be sure we were on the same page." Lana moved her hands back to Court's hips and around to her ass before thrusting into her. "I want this, right here, to be our reality for the rest of our lives."

EPILOGUE

Court had never been happier than she was since moving in with Lana almost seven months earlier. She looked at Lana sitting next to her in the arena where they were watching Eric play in his first Memorial Cup Championship tournament. She took Lana's hand and lifted it to her lips as Eric made a perfect pass to his teammate who in turn shot the puck just over the goalie's blocker to score the game-winning—no, the Memorial Cup–winning—goal.

The crowd erupted as the players swarmed around Eric, who ended up having a tremendous rookie campaign after being called up just ten games into the season. Court couldn't help the pride she felt for him. He'd taken everything she'd tried to teach him to heart, and he'd actually led the league in assists, not only during the regular season, but throughout the playoffs as well.

"You made this possible for him," Lana said into her ear as they hugged each other.

"He did it himself," Court said, shaking her head. They looked out at the ice where Eric and his teammates were still celebrating their win. Eric looked up at them and raised his fist in the air. "He never would have learned anything if he didn't already have it in him."

Court hugged her again, afraid to admit she was trying not to cry. The Wolves hadn't won the championship that year. All things considered, she was happy for Gail because the Warriors had done it again, but Jen Hilton winning the MVP of the playoffs was a bitter pill to swallow. At least she'd gotten the better of Hilton in two separate fights in the final series.

But Eric winning this, today, gave Court the feeling her life had come full circle. Her career as a player was over, but she'd signed on with the Wolves as an assistant coach. She pressed her lips to Lana's temple.

They waited outside the locker room for Eric to emerge. Other players' reunions with their families were fun to watch, but when Eric finally came out, he had a huge smile on his face as he went directly to Lana and gave her a big hug.

"I'm so proud of you, Eric," Lana said. She held on to him tightly as he lifted her off the ground. "Where's your MVP trophy?"

"The staff will get it loaded onto the bus later," he said, pulling Court into a hug once he finally let his mother go. Court was grateful he didn't try lifting her off the ground as well. "I want to thank you for everything you've done for me. I never would have been Rookie of the Year or the MVP of the Cup tourney without you."

"You're welcome," she said as she stepped back, knowing the smile on her face was huge, and not just because of Eric's triumph that day. There were a lot of people hanging around their immediate area, so she took a deep breath and grabbed Lana by the hand. "Can I talk to you both over here for a minute?"

She walked a few feet away and watched the emotions

work their way through Lana's expression. Confusion and worry were the most prominent, but Eric still had an ear-to-ear smile because he knew what was about to happen. He finally urged Lana to come with him to where Court was standing.

"I have a bad feeling," Lana said, looking at Court apprehensively.

"You shouldn't," Court assured her. She took Lana's hands and held them between their bodies. "I just wanted to say something, and there are far too many people over there."

"Well, make it quick," Lana said. "Our dinner reservations are in an hour."

"Lana, two years ago, I didn't even know you," Court said, maintaining eye contact. "A year ago, I had fallen in love with you, and didn't have the guts to tell you. Now, I can't imagine not having you in my life. You've made me so much happier than I ever thought I could be."

Court smiled when Lana wiped a tear from her cheek. Eric handed her the small box she'd asked him to keep until this moment came. After taking a deep breath to try to steady her nerves, she got down on one knee and looked up at Lana, opening the box for her to see the diamond ring inside.

"Yes," Lana said, nodding her head and crying openly now. Court was aware of other people noticing them, but she kept her attention on Lana. "Yes!"

"I didn't even get to ask the question," Court said, her shoulders slumping. "Can you at least let me ask?"

"I'm sorry. Go ahead." Lana clasped her hands in front of her and stood still, waiting.

"Lana Caruso," Court said as she took the ring out of the box and held her hand out for Lana's. "Will you marry me?"

"Can I say yes now?" Lana whispered. Court laughed and got to her feet again as she slid the ring onto Lana's finger.

"Yes, you can answer now."

"Yes, a thousand times," Lana said, holding her hand out in front of her to get a better look at the ring. The crowd gathered a few feet away broke out into cheers, and people were snapping pictures with their phones. Lana looked at Eric, who was standing off to the side, still smiling. "You knew about this and didn't tell me?"

"She said she'd break my kneecaps if I did." Eric shrugged, and Lana looked at Court.

"In my defense, I never actually said I'd do it," Court told her. "I told him I'd have to seriously think about doing it if he let anything slip."

Lana shook her head but stepped closer to Court and put her arms around her neck before kissing her soundly. Court was aware of the crowd cheering again, but it faded away quickly. The woman of her dreams had agreed to be her wife.

"Okay, break it up now," Eric said, obviously embarrassed at the attention they were getting. "I'm starving."

Court broke their kiss and smiled at Lana, then pressed her lips to Lana's nose. "We can continue this in private a little later tonight."

"Deal," Lana said. She slid her arm around Court's waist, and Court's arm went around her shoulders.

Court threw her other arm around Eric's shoulders and they headed for the exit. She'd never allowed herself to dream of having a family of her own, but it was exactly what she had now, and she couldn't be happier.

About the Author

PJ Trebelhorn was born and raised in the greater metropolitan area of Portland, Oregon. Her love of sports (mainly baseball and ice hockey) was fueled in part by her father's interests. She likes to brag about the fact that her uncle managed the Milwaukee Brewers for five years and the Chicago Cubs for one year.

PJ now resides in western New York with her wife, Cheryl, their three cats, and one very neurotic dog. When not writing or reading, PJ enjoys watching movies, playing on the PlayStation, and spending way too much time with stupid games on Facebook. She still roots for the Flyers, Phillies, and Eagles, even though she's now in Sabres and Bills territory.

Books Available From Bold Strokes Books

A Fighting Chance by T. L. Hayes. Will Lou be able to come to terms with her past to give love a fighting chance? (978-1-163555-257-7)

Chosen by Brey Willows. When the choice is adapt or die, can love save us all? (978-1-163555-110-5)

Gnarled Hollow by Charlotte Greene. After they are invited to study a secluded nineteenth-century estate, a former English professor and a group of historians discover that they will have to fight against the unknown if they have any hope of staying alive. (978-1-163555-235-5)

Jacob's Grace by C.P. Rowlands. Captain Tag Becket wants to keep her head down and her past behind her, but her feelings for AJ's second-in-command, Grace Fields, makes keeping secrets next to impossible. (978-1-163555-187-7)

On the Fly by PJ Trebelhorn. Hockey player Courtney Abbott is content with her solitary life until visiting concert violinist Lana Caruso makes her second-guess everything she always thought she wanted. (978-1-163555-255-3)

Passionate Rivals by Radclyffe. Professional rivalry and long-simmering passions create a combustible combination when Emmet McCabe and Sydney Stevens are forced to work together, especially when past attractions won't stay buried. (978-1-63555-231-7)

Proxima Five by Missouri Vaun. When geologist Leah Warren crash-lands on a preindustrial planet and is claimed by its tyrant, Tiago, will clan warrior Keegan's love for Leah give her the strength to defeat him? (978-1-163555-122-8)

Racing Hearts by Dena Blake. When you cross a hot-tempered race car mechanic with a reckless cop, the result can only be spontaneous combustion. (978-1-163555-251-5)

Shadowboxer by Jessica L. Webb. Jordan McAddie is prepared to keep her street kids safe from a dangerous underground protest group, but she isn't prepared for her first love to walk back into her life. (978-1-163555-267-6)

The Tattered Lands by Barbara Ann Wright. As Vandra and Lilani strive to make peace, they slowly fall in love. With mistrust and murder surrounding them, only their faith in each other can keep their plan to save the world from falling apart. (978-1-163555-108-2)

Captive by Donna K. Ford. To escape a human trafficking ring, Greyson Cooper and Olivia Danner become players in a game of deceit and violence. Will their love stand a chance? (978-1-63555-215-7)

Crossing the Line by CF Frizzell. The Mob discovers a nemesis within its ranks, and in the ultimate retaliation, draws Stick McLaughlin from anonymity by threatening everything she holds dear. (978-1-63555-161-7)

Love's Verdict by Carsen Taite. Attorneys Landon Holt and Carly Pachett want the exact same thing: the only open partnership spot at their prestigious criminal defense firm. But will they compromise their careers for love? (978-1-63555-042-9)

Precipice of Doubt by Mardi Alexander & Laurie Eichler. Can Cole Jameson resist her attraction to her boss, veterinarian Jodi Bowman, or will she risk a workplace romance and her heart? (978-1-63555-128-0)

Savage Horizons by CJ Birch. Captain Jordan Kellow's feelings for Lt. Ali Ash have her past and future colliding, setting in motion a series of events that strands her crew in an unknown galaxy thousands of light years from home. (978-1-63555-250-8)

Secrets of the Last Castle by A. Rose Mathieu. When Elizabeth Campbell represents a young man accused of murdering an elderly woman, her investigation leads to an abandoned plantation that reveals many dark Southern secrets. (978-1-63555-240-9)

Take Your Time by VK Powell. A neurotic parrot brings police officer Grace Booker and temporary veterinarian Dr. Dani Wingate together in the tiny town of Pine Cone, but their unexpected attraction keeps the sparks flying. (978-1-63555-130-3)

The Last Seduction by Ronica Black. When you allow true love to elude you once and you desperately regret it, are you brave enough to grab it when it comes around again? (978-1-63555-211-9)

The Shape of You by Georgia Beers. Rebecca McCall doesn't play it safe, but when sexy Spencer Thompson joins her workout class, their nonstop sparring forces her to face her ultimate challenge—a chance at love. (978-1-63555-217-1)

Exposed by MJ Williamz. The closet is no place to live if you want to find true love. (978-1-62639-989-1)

Force of Fire: Toujours a Vous by Ali Vali. Immortals Kendal and Piper welcome their new child and celebrate the defeat of an old enemy, but another ancient evil is about to awaken deep in the jungles of Costa Rica. (978-1-63555-047-4)

Landing Zone by Erin Dutton. Can a career veteran finally discover a love stronger than even her pride? (978-1-63555-199-0)

Love at Last Call by M. Ullrich. Is balancing business, friendship, and love more than any willing woman can handle? (978-1-63555-197-6)

Pleasure Cruise by Yolanda Wallace. Spencer Collins and Amy Donovan have few things in common, but a Caribbean cruise offers both women an unexpected chance to face one of their greatest fears: falling in love. (978-1-63555-219-5)

Running Off Radar by MB Austin. Maji's plans to win Rose back are interrupted when work intrudes, and duty calls her to help a SEAL team stop a Russian mobster from harvesting gold from the bottom of Sitka Sound. (978-1-63555-152-5)

Shadow of the Phoenix by Rebecca Harwell. In the final battle for the fate of Storm's Quarry, even Nadya's and Shay's powers may not be enough. (978-1-63555-181-5)

Take a Chance by D. Jackson Leigh. There's hardly a woman within fifty miles of Pine Cone that veterinarian Trip Beaumont can't charm, except for the irritating new cop, Jamie Grant, who keeps leaving parking tickets on her truck. (978-1-63555-118-1)

Death in Time by Robyn Nyx. Working in the past is hell on your future. (978-1-63555-053-5)

The Outcasts by Alexa Black. Spacebus driver Sue Jones is running from her past. When she crash-lands on a faraway world, the Outcast Kara might be her chance for redemption. (978-1-63555-242-3)

Alias by Cari Hunter. A car crash leaves a woman with no memory and no identity. Together with Detective Bronwen Pryce, she fights to uncover a truth that might just kill them both. (978-1-63555-221-8)

Hers to Protect by Nicole Disney. Ex–high school sweethearts Kaia and Adrienne will have to see past their differences and survive the vengeance of a brutal gang if they want to be together. (978-1-63555-229-4)

Perfect Little Worlds by Clifford Mae Henderson. Lucy can't hold the secret any longer. Twenty-six years ago, her sister did the unthinkable. (978-1-63555-164-8)

Room Service by Fiona Riley. Interior designer Olivia likes stability, but when work brings footloose Savannah into her world and into a new city every month, Olivia must decide if what makes her comfortable is what makes her happy. (978-1-63555-120-4)

Sparks Like Ours by Melissa Brayden. Professional surfers Gia Malone and Elle Britton can't deny their chemistry on and off the beach. But only one can win… (978-1-63555-016-0)

Take My Hand by Missouri Vaun. River Hemsworth arrives in Georgia intent on escaping quickly, but when she crashes her Mercedes into the Clip 'n Curl, sexy Clay Cahill ends up rescuing more than her car. (978-1-63555-104-4)

The Last Time I Saw Her by Kathleen Knowles. Lane Hudson only has twelve days to win back Alison's heart. That is, if she can gather the courage to try. (978-1-63555-067-2)

Wayworn Lovers by Gun Brooke. Will agoraphobic composer Giselle Bonnaire and Tierney Edwards, a wandering soul who can't remain in one place for long, trust in the passionate love destiny hands them? (978-1-62639-995-2)